The NIGHT MARE

Also by Robert Westall

A WALK ON THE WILD SIDE

IF CATS COULD FLY

THE KINGDOM BY THE SEA
Winner of The Guardian
Children's Fiction Award

THE CHRISTMAS CAT

THE CHRISTMAS GHOST

GULF
Shortlisted for
the Whitbread Award,
the Carnegie Medal,
the Federation of Children's Books Award,
the Lancashire Book Award, and
the Sheffield Book Award

FALLING INTO GLORY

ROBERT WESTALL

The NIGHT MARE

METHUEN CHILDREN'S BOOKS

First published in Great Britain 1995 by Methuen Children's Books
an imprint of Reed Consumer Books Limited
Michelin House, 81 Fulham Road, London SW3 6RB
and Auckland, Melbourne, Singapore and Toronto

ISBN 0 416 19075 8

A CIP catalogue record for this book is available
at the British Library

Printed and bound in Great Britain by
Clays Ltd, St Ives plc

Contents

CHAPTER 1

The Chair

Miss Crimond was sitting in Dad's chair, which had once been Grandpa's chair; and Billy hated her.

Grandpa's chair was their best thing. Billy thought it looked like a throne with its great twisted legs that ended in lions' feet, and its great twisted arms that ended in lions' heads, and its back with the coat of arms carved in mahogany on top. Its seat was dark-red velvet, worn almost to threads where people twitched their legs about. But Mam kept it polished so it shone like a new conker.

A throne. And only Dad was allowed to sit in it. Except on Friday night, pay-night, when Miss Crimond came to collect her rents. Then she sat in it, without as much as a by-your-leave, as if it was her right. Like a thin mean queen.

And her younger sister, Miss Helen Crimond, sat in Mam's chair, which was smaller but the second-best thing in that mean, dark, narrow house. Mam's chair had a tapestry seat, all dragons and castles in faded blue and grey; you could get lost dreaming in the pattern. But that was also worn to threads in the front.

'A cup of tea, Miss Crimond?' asked Mam. Her

voice might be weary, but it was the voice of a lady.

'Thank you, Maggie,' said Miss Crimond, as if she was speaking to a servant. And Miss Helen Crimond nodded in agreement. She never did anything but nod in agreement. She reminded Billy of an automaton at a funfair. Billy expected a crazy mechanical laugh to escape her at any moment; though he had a sneaking feeling living with the elder Miss Crimond could not be a lot of fun.

Mam fetched their tea, in the thin, beautiful chipped cups; the only two of the set they had left. Miss Crimond sat sipping, her lips slightly pursed as if the tea was too strong or too weak, with her elbows held in neatly, and her little finger crooked in gentility. And between sips, her eyes roved the room, searching for crumbs on the carpet under the table, or cobwebs on the gas-lamp brackets. The pebble lenses of her gold-rimmed spectacles magnified her eyes, so they looked like fat blue goldfish swimming in bowls too small for them. But those eyes missed nothing.

'We have given the Edmonsons their *notice*,' announced Miss Crimond. 'To be out of their house first thing Monday morning. They have missed paying two weeks' rent. We are *not* a charity. One week behind, I will tolerate. But two weeks is two weeks too many.'

And Miss Helen Crimond gave her marionette nod, never missing a sip of her tea.

'But where will they *go*?' whispered Mam, horrified. 'They've no family to go to . . .'

'That is not our concern. As I said before, we are *not* a charity.'

'Five little bairns,' whispered Mam. 'They'll never send them to the workhouse?'

Even Dad stirred, where he stood with his back to the kitchen range, warming his hands. Billy noticed the cuffs of his suit were frayed again; Mam would have to cut more threads off them. And off the cuffs of his white shirt as well.

'Ben Edmonson's had a bad back,' Dad said in a low voice. 'He's a good worker, but a man can't work with a bad back. And if he can't work, he can't pay rent.'

'They should have saved up for a rainy day,' said Miss Crimond. 'The trouble with that house is *drink*. How often have I seen those children taking empty bottles back to the off-licence?'

And Miss Helen Crimond nodded, putting her empty cup back in her saucer.

But her sister cleared her throat briskly, and reached down into the bulging crocodile-skin bag at her feet. An awful bag, a witch's bag, with the flattened wizened baby crocodile's head sticking out of one side of it, and its flattened wizened four tiny legs sticking out of the other. Billy had a fascinated dread of that bag. What other things of power and evil did it contain?

But on this occasion, she only produced her little grey account-book and posh fountain pen.

Dad reached into his trouser pocket with an incoherent grunt and produced two big shiny half-crowns, for the rent. It was a moment of terror for Billy, until those two half-crowns appeared. Dad was a fool with his money and if, one of these Friday nights, those two half-crowns did not appear, then Miss Crimond would put them out on the street as well. In a little huddled island of their furniture in the rain, with neighbours gossiping to see what they had, and the kids from the next street jeering from a distance, or even running past to throw stones at their mirror to get them seven years' more bad luck.

'Thank you, Mr Leggett,' said Miss Crimond, strict as if she was a headmistress and Dad had just escaped a caning. She wrote in her little grey book, and then in the pink rent-book that Mam produced from behind the broken Staffordshire figure of Lord Nelson on the mantelpiece.

'And the Murgatroyds had better watch their p's and q's as well,' said Miss Crimond like a judge. 'Or they'll be out on the street as well. I've been told she had washing hanging out till Thursday last week, and her front step is filthy and that door-knocker hasn't seen polish for a month. This is a *respectable* street. It was always respectable in my father's time, and I owe it to his memory to keep it that way.' She gathered up her gloves, and glanced at the clock: Grandpa's clock where it hung on the wall. 'Is that the right time? We must be going.'

But alas, it was never the right time. Except twice in every twenty-four hours. Grandpa's clock, for all its shining brass and turned pillars, and the proud eagle on top, had long since stopped, and there wasn't the money to have it mended. Its ornate gilded pendulum hung motionless for all to see, bereft of life. But every week Miss Crimond asked if that was the right time, and listened with her grey head cocked while poor Mam mumbled out some garbled excuse. Grandpa's clock was their third-best thing; three feet high and something to be proud of, but Miss Crimond turned it into a thing of torture, of shame. Like the Edmonsons' beer bottles and the Murgatroyds' unpolished door-knocker . . .

Mam showed the Misses Crimond to the front door. Dad flung himself savagely down in Grandpa's chair, as the door closed behind them.

'One day I'll strangle that woman. Patronising bitch! Giving themselves airs and graces, just because they own this street. My father could have bought them up ten times over. Twenty times! Fifty times over!'

'For God's sake, William, don't start that again,' said Mam in a weary voice, as she came back in. 'What's past is past. Your father's dead and buried, a long time ago. Give us a bit of peace.'

'But my father had no *right* . . .' Dad's voice was raised in its usual squeal of self-pity.

Billy closed his eyes. He knew the story off by heart. Grandpa had been rich; the richest man in town. Dad and Uncle Horace and Uncle George had all gone to public school. But when Grandpa died, he'd left his fleet of collier-brigs to Uncle Horace, because he was adventurous. And left his coal-carts to Uncle George who was hardworking. But to Dad, who'd been much too fond of riding horses and betting on them, and shooting all manner of birds and beasts and generally having a good time, he'd left . . .

'This damned chair,' groaned Dad in agony. 'This damn-blasted chair. He told me on his deathbed.

He said I had to learn the value of money the hard way.'

Worse, Uncle George had prospered exceedingly and had a grand house in Newcastle, and was an alderman on the city council. And Uncle Horace had prospered exceedingly, and moved to a grand house in Tynemouth, and was on the town council. And Dad was a clerk in the pay-office at Smith's Dock, earning two guineas a week, and they lived in Back Tennyson Street. They never saw Uncle Horace and Uncle George any more, except at family funerals, and then all they did was Talk Big about how much money they had, and how much more they were going to make.

'A cup of tea, dear?' asked Mam timidly. This was the crucial moment. If Dad said yes, he would just sit there and moan with his head in his hands for an hour, and then pick up the evening paper or a bit of his fretwork. But if he said no, he would go out for a drink of something stronger, with a whole week's wages in his pocket, and meet his scrounging mates, and not stagger home till ten when the pubs closed. And then he was not good old Dad any more but a raging devil, so that Billy had to be tucked up safe in bed and pretending to be asleep, and Mam too. And they would lie and listen to the sounds downstairs of Dad crashing into things and cursing, till finally there would be a thump and snores. And then Mam would know it was safe to tiptoe down, and rifle Dad's pockets of what money he had left; and put on her coat and slip to the corner shop, which would still be open, and spend the money quick on groceries, so they would have something to eat next week. And Dad would wake up with a terrible hangover and all shamefaced that he'd spent all his week's wages on booze, and never even ask where next week's meals had come from.

'Aye,' said Dad with a profound sigh coming through his hands. 'Aye, a cup of tea. Aah suppose so.'

And Mam and Billy gave each other a quick grin of relief, that they wouldn't have to take Grandpa's clock to the pawnshop this week. And Miss Crimond would get her half-crowns as usual next Friday.

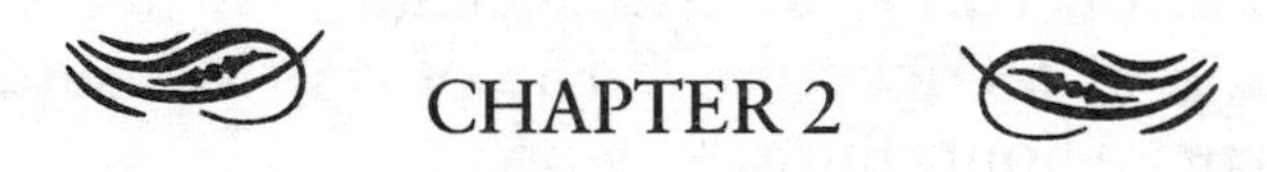

CHAPTER 2

Cricket

Just then came a strange sort of howl from outside the back door. Which could be made out with some difficulty as 'Billy-oh! Billy-oh!'

Mam twitched the curtain. 'It's Albert Snowdon. Shall I tell him you're out?'

Albert Snowdon never knocked. Knocking was for grown-ups. If you knocked on your mate's door, your mate's mother might come instead, which he found very embarrassing. You might have disturbed your mate's mother in the middle of her cooking or cleaning; she might give you a clip round the ear. Albert was a pessimist in that direction. So he just stood at the back door and shouted, 'Billy-oh,' in a low voice for hours. Sometimes he simply stood patiently in silence, waiting for someone to come. He had been known, after dark, to give someone's mother a serious turn, standing there on the step like Count Dracula.

'What's he got in his hand?' asked Billy cautiously.

'A ball,' said Mam. 'A sort of cricket ball.'

'A BALL?' Albert Snowdon with empty hands was at best a burden. But Albert Snowdon with a new ball was a sort of Second Coming. Nobody had

had a ball of any description for a week. Cricket, soccer, off-coming-away were all possible now. Life in the ball-less street could begin again. Billy was out of the back door like greased lightning.

It wasn't really a cricket ball, but a cheap imitation of a cricket ball. They'd probably kick it to bits in an hour. But why worry?

'Where'dya gettit?'

'Bought it,' said Albert proudly. 'Threepence at Thompson's.'

'Where'd *you* get threepence?' Threepence was three weeks' pocket-money.

'Mr Murray down the road gave me a penny, to take a parcel to Mr Fraggle.'

'Mr *who*?'

'Fraggle.'

'Where does he live?'

'Mr Murray didn't know. He just said, "Somewhere round here." I had to go to doors to ask.'

'Never heard of him.'

'Nobody else had, either. They just kept laughing. But one or two gave me a ha'penny or a farthing. I think they were sorry for me. An' it's pay-night.'

'I think Mr Murray was having you on, Albert. I don't think there *is* a Mr Fraggle.'

'Yes, there is,' said Albert stoutly. 'His name's on the box.'

He held up a small cardboard box he'd been holding behind his back in his other hand. 'There's his name, see!'

The box was quite clearly labelled FRAGILE in red letters on white.

'We can have a game now,' said Albert coaxingly.

'If you can help me find Mr Fraggle. He could be waiting for it. It could be serious. It's *heavy.*'

'Give us it here.' Billy tore open the box. It was full of rubbish; a broken cup and saucer, three large rusty nuts and bolts and a lump of lead pipe.

'Perhaps Mr Fraggle's got a second-hand shop?' said Albert hopefully.

As soon as news of the ball got about, the gang gathered swiftly. Sam Spode was little, which was just as well, for he was always after being leader of the gang. He had a lot of bright ideas, but if he got too uppity, Billy could always bash him into submission. But he had to be watched. With his long long shorts, that çame well below his knees, his strong bandy legs ending in ragged plimsolls that had once been white, but were now stained by sweat and dust to khaki; his fringe of hair falling nearly into his eyes, and his habit of gritting his teeth even while talking, he had the air of a ferocious mongrel terrier waiting to bite the postman.

Nathaniel Diggins fancied being gang-leader too. He was the best fighter; also he could be persuaded, after a lot of argument, to deal with people who needed dealing with. He was tall and reckoned he was good-looking. The girls in their class said he was the boy they'd most like to meet up a dark alley one night. But he was as reluctant with girls as he was with fighting. In the end, he was lazy, and soon lost interest in anything, which was fortunate for Billy.

Henry Small, though, was the main reason why Billy was gang boss. Henry was middle-sized and plump and faithful to Billy. However horrible Billy was, Henry always came back for more. Henry wasn't much given to thinking: he let Billy do his thinking for him; it saved the bother.

It took the combined efforts of Henry Small, Nathaniel Diggins and Sam Spode to convince Albert that Mr Fraggle did not exist. Albert had a very trusting nature. In the end they settled it by leaving the box on Mr Murray's front doorstep. Nat and Sam did up the parcel again, and slipped in several ripe bits of dog-dirt while Albert was distracted. As Billy pointed out, if you let grown-ups get away with pulling a trick like that unpunished, a kid's life wouldn't be worth living.

It wasn't real cricket, because they only had one batsman, a bowler, a wicket-keeper and two fielders. They took turns at going in to bat, and the one with the highest scores at the end won. And they had to play in the front street, because the back lanes were too narrow and full of tom-cats, dustbins and housewives standing outside their back gates gossiping, and other such obstacles. But the front street was quite convenient. No car or lorry ever came down Back Tennyson Street, and the odd horse and cart only made the game more interesting. Except the time the greengrocer's horse ate the ball, and the greengrocer wouldn't cough up the price of a new one. He even said if the horse got a blockage and died, *he* would charge *them* for a new horse. But the beast was still hale and hearty; though they looked through the horse's droppings in vain for any trace of their ball, following it around for two days non-stop.

At first, they had used a round cast-iron manhole cover as the wicket, but then people who were bowled out said the ball had been too high, and the arguments lasted for hours. So Sam Spode's dad had set three bits of broom-handle in a plank of wood; only he had stuck them in with glue so well, and the plank was so big, that you had to knock the whole thing over before anyone would admit to being out.

The bat belonged to Albert. It was so bound round with black sticky tape that hardly any wood was visible. Only the bit which Albert said had been personally signed for his dad by Dr W. G. Grace. But since it had faded and been inked back in many times, and now read 'W. J. Grace' this was not believed. As Billy said, if Dr Grace didn't know how to spell his own name . . .

Albert played the role of the good doctor, as usual. Billy chose the role of Jack Hobbs, Sam was Sutcliffe, and Nat said he was Harold Larwood, because he was the best bowler. They let Albert have first bat, because it was his bat and ball, and he always got out quick anyway, because he was an awful batsman. Unlike the good doctor, who only closed one eye, Albert closed both and swiped blindly. He never hit the ball, but had been known to knock the whole wicket over.

If you put the ball in somebody's front garden, you were six-and-out. People were quite decent about the ball going into their gardens. You had to look up at old Mrs Turpin's bedroom window, and she was always there, spying round her curtains, and she would nod and bob her head and smile, and then you could open her gate and fetch the ball. And somehow Mr Miller would always come out and cut his hedge when a game was going on. He liked to catch the ball, with a neat flick of the wrist, if it came his way, and shout, 'Howzat?' Billy thought that, given any encouragement at all, he'd come over and join in the game. A real king of the kids, Mr Miller.

Everyone was decent, except Miss Crimond. She confiscated any balls that went into her garden; which was why there was such a shortage of balls in the street. She was so mean she even kept the confiscated balls in a row on her inside windowsill, where everyone could see them and yearn for lost pocket-money and eat their hearts out. When she saw a game in progress she would often come into her front garden and indicate the balls in her window and smile an evil smile . . . They would have liked to play even further off down the street, but it was cobbled there, and the balls flew in all directions when they bounced. They had learned to be careful, except Albert and he never hit the ball anyway . . .

Except today; he closed both eyes, took a swipe that spun him round in a full circle, and connected.

Sam Spode got despairing fingertips to it, but it still flew like a bird, straight for Miss Crimond's hedge.

And lodged on top. Tantalisingly still reachable, still in the land of the living. It lay there glistening in the sun, on top of the low, low hedge.

Billy ran like he'd never run before. He heard rather than saw Miss Crimond's front door fly open. His eyes were on the ball. Ten feet, five feet away. Still there. Two feet, one foot. His hand closed over the ball and then Miss Crimond's hand closed over his, like the talons of a vulture.

'Give me that ball!'

They pushed and pulled each other across the hedge. Billy would not let go of the ball, and Miss Crimond would not let go of Billy's hand. Her nails were digging into him . . .

He realised half the street had come out to watch. It gave him an idea.

'Ow, help, Mam!' he shouted. 'She's twisting my hand. She's got her claws into me. I'm *bleeding*!' Without further ado, he burst into tears. It was a trick he had; it was useful in school, when there was a chance you might get caned.

Miss Crimond didn't believe him; but she knew the watching street did. She hesitated . . . and he was suddenly gone. Running down the street with the ball, grinning at his mates, where Miss Crimond couldn't see.

She went in and slammed her front door.

They held a hurried conference.

'Better pack up,' said Sam Spode. 'She'll be watching every move we make. Sharper than an umpire.'

'Go on,' said Billy. 'We can play soft ones along the ground.'

'Not Albert, he can't.'

'Albert's six-and-out.'

'No, I'm not,' said Albert. 'Ball didn't go in her garden. I ran twenty-four while you were wrestling with her.'

'Six-and-out,' said Billy threateningly and finally.

They all nodded.

'Give us me bat, then,' said Albert. 'Aah'm going home for me supper.'

Wiser counsels prevailed.

'Let him stay in and be twenty-four, Billy. He'll never hit it again. Not twice in one night.'

Harold Larwood bowled a real killer body-liner.

Albert shut both eyes, swung . . .

And hit it again. High, high in the air. Miss Crimond's door opened. She walked out, it seemed quite casually. Stood waiting with her hand raised. The ball went straight to it like a bird to its nest.

'May as well go an' have your supper, then, Albert,' said Billy bitterly.

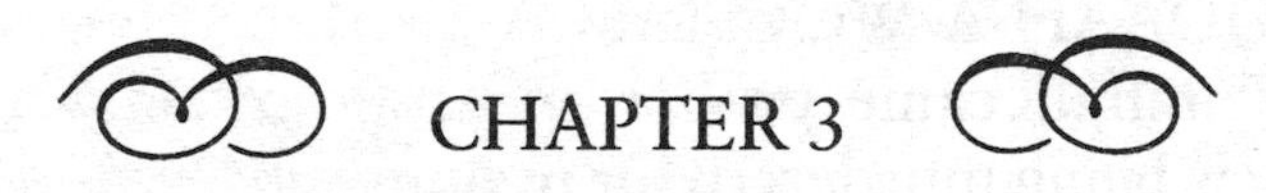

CHAPTER 3

The Lamp

They always met at their streetlamp after dark; after that marvellous moment when the old lamplighter they called 'Tin-Tash' pulled down with his long pole, and the gas-mantles glared dull red, then bright yellow, then dazzling white, and when you looked at the world again, it was suddenly and magically night. The day had gone, taking school, mental arithmetic and bossy, sharp-eyed grown-ups with it, and substituted mysterious shadows, black tom-cats and wonder. The sweet-shop window glowed like the jewel-box it truly was; the stars swung out from behind the black chimney-pots to be argued over, and mothers' voices lost all authority, and enquired timorously, 'Who's there?' The night belonged to the boys, and any girl crazy enough to want her pigtails pulled and the colour of her knickers enquired after.

The streetlamp summoned them from afar, turned into a lighted tent, enclosing them not just in light, but in warmth too. For, turning up their faces, they could imagine the faint heat of the gas mantles giving them sunburn. And there were little black caverns at the base of the lamp, where secret coded messages could be left, if you didn't mind your hand smelling of dog-pee afterwards. Or you could hang old bicycle tyres over the lamp's outstretched iron arms, and swing like Tarzan of the Apes, shouting, 'A-WOOAAH-A-WOOAAH-A-WOOAAH,' until Mrs Threlfall came to her front door to enquire who was being murdered. Or if, wonder of wonders, you could find an abandoned coil of sodden rope in the gutter, you suddenly had a free roundabout that swung you wildly round and round the lamp, till you let go at the very point where the twisting rope snatched to trap your fingers and you landed with a clatter and spark of heel-plates in the middle of Mrs Threlfall's privet hedge.

They sat on the kerb, in a cursing straggle.

'Should be a law against it . . .'

'There is a law against it. It's *thieving*.'

'All right, clevercuts. Go an' fetch a policeman then!'

'Why don't they go an' live down Tynemouth? They've got pots o' money. Why don't they go an' live wi' their own sort? An' leave us in peace? They could have electric light and flush toilet an' everything. I'd go an' live down Tynemouth, if I had the money. So would me dad.'

'This street was left to me by my father.' Sam mimicked Miss Crimond to perfection. 'I shall stay and see it remains *respectable*.'

'Very funny,' said Billy. 'Har har. Don't ring us, we'll ring you.' That was a joke about telephones he'd heard when Mam and Dad took him as a treat to the music hall. He wasn't quite sure why everyone thought it was so funny, at the music hall, but he liked to say it anyway. It sounded smart and worldly.

'If they knew how much everybody hated them, they'd pack up an' go tomorrow,' said Nat. 'People are really mad at them, about them going to chuck the Edmonsons out.'

'But people don't dare *show* it,' said Henry Small. 'Otherwise they'd get chucked out of their houses too.'

'We need a plan,' said Billy darkly. 'A plan of campaign.'

 CHAPTER 4 

The Telephone

Saturday morning, a *fine* Saturday morning, was usually the best time in the week. But they still sat on the kerb, arguing; they still hadn't worked out a plan of campaign. And they were getting more fed up by the minute. Especially with Billy, who was their leader, and who *should* have come up with a plan of campaign. And who could think of nothing except knocking other people's plans to pieces.

'We could wait till night an' tie a long black thread to their doorknocker . . .' said Nat.

'Kids' stuff,' said Billy. Knockers were just a joke; they even did that to people they quite liked, like Mr Miller. Kids had always done that.

'We could put glue in their keyhole . . .' said Henry.

'Tube of glue costs tuppence,' said Billy. They had the money; they even had enough between them for a new ball; it was the morning after pay-day . . . but they hadn't the heart. They just knew that any ball they bought would be decorating the inside of Miss Crimond's windowsill within half an hour.

'We could phone up the livery stables and order

ten tons of manure to be dumped at their back gate,' said Sam. 'I've got the livery stables' number. It's on the sides of all their carts.'

'And you've got a telephone, of course,' said Billy. 'Your family's so rich they've *all* got phones.'

'Oh, har,' said Sam dismally. Only very rich people had phones. The only public phone was inside the post office, and the counter-clerks would never let kids near that.

'Why don't they go an' live with their own sort?' bleated Albert. It wasn't even his own idea; it was somebody else's idea from last night, which he'd saved up to reuse, being desperately short of ideas of his own. 'They're rich enough,' he added, greatly daring, before somebody kicked his leg.

'They're rich enough,' said Billy. 'But they want to stay here and go on like Kaiser Bill, bullying people. They'd be bored out of their minds down Tynemouth, with no one to bully. Oh, blast, I wish *I* was rich, like me Grandpa . . .'

'Rich?' asked Sam in amazement. '*Your* family? Rich?'

Billy cursed inwardly. Grandpa's riches must never be mentioned outside the family. It was not that the neighbours didn't know about Grandpa's riches, but they had forgotten about them, and in the hurly-burly of life, no longer thought about them. And Mam said it was best to let sleeping dogs lie. Nasty things had happened when their family first came to live down here, eight years ago. Toffs who had come down in the world had been fair game for the wrath of the workers. Dad's briefcase had been stolen, when he left it for only a moment on the front step one evening, and thrown into the river. The police brought it back a fornight later, ruined. When Mam had hung out her washing in the back lane along with all the other mothers', dog-dirt had been thrown at it. There were a thousand ways neighbours could punish you, if they thought you were being uppity, giving yourself airs. Mam and Dad still talked posher in the house than they ever dared talk outside. And, after a few cruel tormentings, Billy had long ago learnt to do the same.

But now the whole gang was looking at him. With a growing air of derision. They'd been fed up with him already, and they were just looking for someone to pick on besides Albert; they were tired of picking on Albert. But a new victim . . . Billy felt his control of the gang, always precarious, really starting to slip.

So he swore them to darkest secrecy, and told them the whole story. Certainly he got all their attention, till he'd finished. But when he stopped, Sam said, 'It's a pack of lies. You're just having us on.'

Billy contemplated beating Sam up. But a fight would really break the gang up, and he'd be out on his neck. And once the other gangs in the neighbourhood knew his gang was broken up, and Billy was alone, there would be a large number of old scores to pay off. Weeks of agony; endless misery.

'Where was this grand house of your grandpa's then?' said Nat, openly sneering.

'Preston Park. So there! It was called The Elms.'

'Show us, then,' said Nat. He was getting very bold.

'Right, I will,' said Billy, with more conviction than he felt. For he had no memory of ever going to The Elms; Grandpa had died when he was three. The only memories Billy had of him were of a long white beard, a bald head and the smell of tobacco on his breath. Billy had only a vague idea where Preston Park was; on the far side of Preston Cemetery. And no idea of where the house lay within Preston Park . . .

'Right, come on, then,' said Nat, grinning mockingly. The rest got to their feet, suddenly interested. At least they were going somewhere, and the chance to take the mickey out of Billy looked really promising.

It was a long way to Preston Park, and the late October sun turned surprisingly hot. Just before Preston Cemetery there was a shop that sold large red and green bottles of pop for threepence, with a halfpenny back on the bottle. A row broke out about whether the gang should blue their combined pocket-money on one. Billy despaired. Anarchy was breaking out all over. They trailed after him along the cemetery wall, still arguing about the pop and not consulting him at all. Albert, at the very back, kept on asking how much further and complaining his feet hurt. Billy kept looking sideways at the tall, white, marble angels that poked over the railings, and thinking it might be quite peaceful to be dead . . .

And then they were at the entrance to Preston

Park and suddenly Billy remembered the huge lawn in the middle of the square of houses, with its posh cast-iron benches and tennis-court, and railings to keep out the general public. He also suddenly and miraculously remembered that The Elms was halfway up the road on the far side of the square. So he confidently led them up to it.

Or rather to a closed pair of iron gates, an immaculate drive winding away into shady darkness, a lot of elm trees still with most of their leaves, and a couple of large black chimneys looming over all. Still, there was a carved wooden sign, only slightly leaning, that grandly pronounced in gilded letters 'THE ELMS'.

'There! So!'

The gang were not impressed.

'Not much for a two-mile walk,' said Nat nastily. 'Doesn't *prove* anything.'

'What you expect? Dancing girls?' Billy was outraged. 'I only said me grandpa *used* to live there. I expect somebody else lives there now.'

'*Yeah*,' said Henry, who was normally Billy's staunchest supporter, and he laughed openly.

Billy was desperate. He knew the mood they were in. They would buy the bottle of pop between them, and not share it with him. They would snipe at him all the hot road back, and by the time they reached home, he would no longer amount to anything. It was not to be borne. *Anything* was better than that.

So he took a suicidal decision, put his hand on the closed gate, and said casually, 'I'll show you round if you like. I'll bet Grandpa's old servants still remember me. He only died eight years ago.'

That shook them. Four mouths agape. Before Nat had finished, 'You wouldn't dare . . .' Billy had pressed down the iron latch and strolled through.

'Close the gate behind you, Albert,' he called back, with the cool voice of aristocracy.

Billy strode ahead, walking almost on tiptoe, every sense at top pitch, like the silent cowboy heroes of the movies. He could almost *hear* the cinema pianist rolling out her dramatic danger music . . . the rest of them he could hear trailing behind him like sheep, talking in low impressed whispers.

There was a sudden patch of sunlight by the drive, as the crowding elms gave back. There was a white statue there, life-size, of a woman, on a marble plinth. From a quick glance, Billy reckoned it was the young Queen Victoria, with green algae streaming down her from her time in the woods. But he waved his hand grandly in its direction and said, 'My grandmother . . . as a young woman. I'm glad they've kept that. But she could do with a good scrub-down. I must speak to them about that.'

Then the elms were thinning, and green lawns coming into view. Far across them, a tall, thin gardener had his back to Billy's party, chopping the edge of the lawn straight with his spade. He was making so much noise, he hadn't heard their footsteps. Dear God, let him not turn round and see them. He'd chuck them out with ignominy . . .

'Hey, Billy,' yelled Albert from the back. 'Do you know *that* feller?'

Billy could have screamed as the gardener turned and noticed them, and began to walk across. But he gave a lordly wave to the gardener, and shouted, 'Good morning,' in the way toffs did, across miles and miles. Then he turned and snarled at his troops, 'Say good morning to the gardener. Where's your manners?'

They followed him like the sheep they were. 'Good morning,' they called in cheery voices, and waved merrily.

It baffled the gardener. If they'd turned to run, he'd have known what to do with them. But . . . he began walking along his borders slowly, keeping a wary eye on them, but reluctant to poke his nose in and bring trouble on himself.

Time was running out. They were nearing the great grey house, with its pillared portico and three floors of shining windows. With its great black double doors and shining brass bellpush, with the little white porcelain button in the middle, marked 'PRESS'.

What else could Billy do? Somewhere, inside the house, the bell jangled. There were female footsteps on the tiled floor, getting nearer and nearer.

Then a lady was standing there, in a long black dress and white starched pinafore. She had grey hair piled up on top of her head, and somehow was much too important for a maid, though certainly not a member of the family. And Billy felt she was at ease, as if none of the family was there. And she had a kind though lined face, and a little ghost of a smile to see them standing there. Billy just knew she was one of the right sort.

'Good morning,' he said, risking all. 'My name is William Leggett, and my grandfather used to live here.' And gave her his wide-eyed open look, the one that had sometimes stopped the Head caning him.

But he could never have even hoped for the reaction he got.

She bent down and hugged him.

'Lord love yer, Master William,' she said. 'The last time I saw you, you were scarce out of swaddling-clothes. What a big lad you've grown.'

It had been a morning of wonders. First she had dismissed the lurking gardener with a grand, 'That will be all, Bates!' Then she had led them on a tour of the house, where all the furniture was draped with pale covers, so it looked like herds of ghostly cattle in the darkness of lowered blinds. Because the family had gone to Mentone for the winter. They had been shown the potted palms that Grandpa had installed years before in the conservatory, the hallstand with the fencing sword he had used as a young man, slim and sinister among the present family's walking sticks. They had seen his books still in the library, most of them, ('A great reader he was, your grandfather, Master William.') and even his portrait, complete with bald head and white beard and robes of office as Lord Mayor of Newcastle. ('It was so big your uncles didn't want it, and the present family bought it, 'cos taking it away would've left too big a hole in the decorations.')

Now they were sitting in the kitchen with Mrs Mallory, Mrs Marjorie Mallory, who told them she was the housekeeper and had been housekeeper to Grandpa before that. And she had summoned a neat little maid in cap and apron, and had lots of home-made lemonade brought.

Billy looked round his assembled troops. They sat ill at ease, dazed, drinking their lemonade, all trace of rebellion utterly crushed. The risk had been worth it, well worth it. At least they all sat there except Sam, who, delightfully blushing, had asked permission to go to the toilet.

'I hope he hasn't got lost,' said Mrs Marjorie Mallory, 'or pulled the chain too soon and gone down to the river.'

'He has a little trouble with . . .' said Billy apologetically.

Mrs Mallory nodded sympathetically. 'I've had bother that way all my life. My mother always said kidneys would be the death of me, and of her, though she's still hale and hearty at seventy-eight.'

But, underneath, Billy was cursing. That little sneak Sam Spode was definitely up to something. Mucking about with Grandpa's rapier, or mucking about with Grandpa's potted palms. Sneaky little Spode didn't fool him for a moment. If he did anything, Billy would wring his sodding little neck . . .

'I think we'd better be going,' Billy said. 'We can pick up poor little Sam on the way.'

And indeed there was the sound of flushing as they passed the great mahogany door of the servants' WC, and Sam emerged saying, 'It's got a little handle at the side you pull. Like the brake on a cart.'

'They haven't got a flush lav at home,' explained Billy viciously. 'But his father's a good honest worker.'

'We can't all have flush toilets, can we?' said Mrs Mallory understandingly. 'You must come again. Perhaps the gardener can find some little jobs for you boys to do. Weeding, perhaps?'

Sam Spode nodded vigorously. 'Any time, missus. Any time for a nice lady like you.' Little sneaking creep . . .

The door had scarcely closed before Billy had Sam by the throat, strangling him in a quiet death-grip with his own tie.

'What you do? Wotcher nick? I'll kill you, Spode.'

'Let go his throat,' said Nat. 'How can he tell us while you're choking him?'

Sam took several lungfulls of air, then grinned and said, 'I've ordered five tons of manure from the livery stables. For Miss Crimond. Up her back entry. After dark tonight. And don't make any noise that will disturb the neighbours.'

'You *what*?'

'Didn't you notice the telephone in their library?'

Billy didn't know whether to slap him on the back or strangle him afresh.

CHAPTER 5

Let Battle Commence

'And in that last day,' thundered the Vicar, 'the Lord shall descend in glory with all His angels, and he shall put the goats on His left hand, and the sheep on His right, and the righteous shall be lifted up into the air, and the wicked cast down into hell . . . '

Billy's mind was full of an enormous vision, of a celestial traffic jam, a sort of Piccadilly Circus in the rush hour like he'd seen on the picture postcard his Aunt Millie had once sent them from a holiday in London. Angels descending, the righteous ascending, goats dashing to the right and sheep to the left, and the Lord waving his white-clad arms like a demented policeman on point-duty. He giggled.

Mam poked him hard in the ribs and said, 'You haven't lost your penny, have you?'

He came down to earth with a bump as the Vicar announced the closing hymn, and the congregation, quite calm through the Vicar's vision of the Final Judgement, showed acute anxiety about finding the pennies and threepenny pieces stowed away inside their best clean Sunday gloves. Again, Billy looked round for the Misses Crimond, but they only came to Evensong, where there were no kids.

It was only a short walk back from church. For some reason best known to Mam, they always left for church by the front door and came home by the back, duty done.

They turned into the back lane and . . .

It was not just a hill of manure; it was a Mount Everest of manure. It blocked the back lane from one side to the other, and piled up six feet high against the Misses Crimond's back gate. Some of it was still steaming in the bright October sunlight and the frosty October air. It gave the heap the menacing feel of a just-slumbering equine volcano. The odd surviving bluebottle, to whom the heap must have resembled paradise, buzzed and settled lazily. On the walls of the lane, on every rooftop, sparrows gathered cheeping at the sight of such bounty.

The smell, though not unpleasant, was very ripe. Billy was just glad Sam hadn't ordered cow manure, or pig.

All the neighbours had gathered too, men in their shirt-sleeves without collars, nursing hangovers. Women in black shawls.

'Disgraceful!'

'What can they want it for?'

'It's a public-health hazard!'

'Somebody should tell the council!'

'It's a practical joke,' said old Toddser Brown. 'I've seen it done many a time, to people folk didn't like.' He raised his ancient quavery voice. 'Hey, Miss Crimond, somebody's left you an early Christmas box.'

The cry was taken up by many voices, louder and

louder, more and more gleefully. Steps were heard coming down the Misses Crimond's yard. Their back gate was snatched open.

'Whoever is causing a riot on the Lord's Day?' thundered Miss Crimond, with such godly righteousness that the crowd quailed back. Even though her grey hair was just showing above the pile.

At that moment, the heap slid, burying her to the waist. Behind her, buried to her knees, her sister screamed.

Billy had never heard adults laugh so much. They didn't usually have much to laugh about. People had to lean against walls, hold each other up.

'I shall send for the police,' screeched Miss Crimond.

The crowd fell sulkily silent.

'Who has *dared* do this? This is adults, not children! And when the police find the culprit, they will be put out of hearth and home and I will personally see they will never rent another house in this town!' Miss Crimond's eagle eye searched every face, but since every face was innocent, she got no satisfaction.

'Police won't shift this lot for you!' muttered a man's voice from the back of the crowd.

'Who said that?' thundered Miss Crimond. But there was no reply to such a silly question.

But it seemed Miss Crimond had suddenly realised the size of her problem, and that the police indeed could not deal with it. And she was no mean fighter. A smile that was almost gracious, certainly condescending, was forced across her face.

'This manure is a gift to the neighbourhood,' she announced. 'Until lunchtime, anyone can have as much as they like, *free*!'

The crowd murmured. The stuff was much prized. They all had little front gardens, and most had built a long narrow garden in their grim back yards, laboriously carting soil for miles from the countryside around the town, where their grandfathers had once lived. They always rushed out with buckets and shovels every time a horse passed, almost fighting for its droppings. Now, they rushed home and brought old coalsacks and buckets, and even unwanted prams that still had four wheels. They rushed to their allotments down by the railway cuttings to fetch their wheelbarrows and watering-cans. Words spread from street to street about the bounty, like wildfire. Folk were even seen, near lunchtime, from the far side of town, so fast does good news travel.

By one o'clock, the last of the public-health hazard was being carefully swept up in dustpans.

'Aye, well, it was good while it lasted,' sighed Sam to Billy, under his breath, as they watched. 'Next time I'll order coal. She'll not give coal away!'

They went back to The Elms the next Saturday. They had a lovely time sweeping up elm leaves and made a great bonfire, and danced round it, much to the consternation of the gardener, waving their assorted rakes in the air and nearly doing each other serious injuries.

But Mrs Marjorie Mallory, snug in her fur hat and furred muff and sprigged top coat, just smiled and said boys would be boys.

And then Sam Spode walked across to her, his hand up in the air and blushing charmingly with embarrassment, to ask, 'Can I go to the lavvy, miss?'

'I worry about that child,' said Mrs Mallory, as he departed briskly. 'Is there nothing the doctors can do?'

'I don't think he'll make old bones,' said Billy sadly and piously.

On the way home, he took Sam by the throat again. 'If you sodding well get caught you'll ruin everything. Threepence each we got today *and* a big mug of cocoa. And early mince-pies. Who else gets mince-pies this early?'

And the gang, even Nat, muttered in agreement. They were on to a good thing, and they knew it. Even though Albert said, grudgingly, 'Perhaps they were *late* mince-pies. From last Christmas. I think there was a bit of mould on mine.'

'There's not just Mrs Mallory to dodge, you know,' stormed Billy. 'There's the maid an' the footman an' all.'

'I know,' said Sam, with a smirk. 'They were both in the butler's pantry, kissing each other. They didn't even notice when I walked past. They always do that when Mrs Mallory's in the garden. Lost to the world. Young love . . .'

'Why were you so long? You were *ages*.'

'I rang up three coal merchants. Including your uncle's.'

Billy felt like punching him in the belly. Where it hurt most.

Miss Crimond caught the first coalman, as he

dumped his first sack through her coal hatch. They had a right barney, the neighbours reported. But he refused to take away that first sack even for her, and she had to pay him two shillings. When he alleged she'd ordered twenty bags, she put on her coat and went down to the police station with her sister to make a formal complaint.

While they were away, the second coalman delivered. He piled coal nearly to the coalhouse ceiling and went away. The weight of coal made the coalhouse door collapse, spilling most of the coal out across their back yard.

Which left plenty of room for the third coalman to empty his twenty bags . . .

When they got back, the neighbours reported Miss Helen Crimond had hysterics, and Miss Crimond had to slap her back to sanity.

There were no offers of free coal to the neighbourhood, even though the Misses Crimond couldn't get out the back gate to their dustbins.

But the next Friday night, Miss Crimond announced she was putting up all rents by two shillings a week – everyone knew it was to pay for the coal.

The next Saturday morning, they sat grumbling on the kerb. Everybody's pocket-money had been stopped for good. Nobody had a roast joint for the weekend, or a cake for Sunday tea. All trips to the cinema, known officially as the Howard Hall and unofficially as the Fleapit, were cancelled for the foreseeable future. In fact, the future stretched away treatless and barren, right up to the shores of Christmas itself.

'Bread an' scrape for Sunday tea,' moaned Nat.

'Us aren't havin' any Christmas presents this year,' moaned Henry.

'All your fault,' said Billy, and kicked Sam's outstretched leg. 'You and your bloody bright ideas. *And* they're still there, wi' coal to last them a twelvemonth, all for free. We'll never shift them now.'

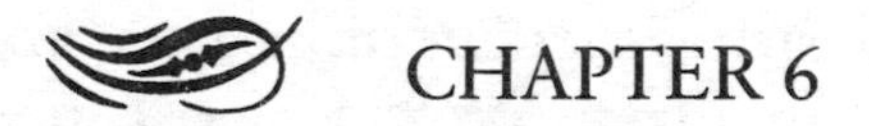 CHAPTER 6 

The Match

They waited in Billy's yard for the football match to start, for they hadn't a bean between them. They might, like luckier boys, have parked their bicyles against the sagging tarred fencing of Appleby Park, and stood on their saddles and watched the match over the top, free, at least till the man came. But they had no bikes. They might, like others, have bored holes with a brace-and-bit in the timber fence itself. But they could no longer lay hands on a brace-and-bit. Dads had become too wary. So all they could do was sit patiently in Billy's yard, and listen to the crowd's bellow coming through the warm muggy autumn air, like the distant roaring of an enormous lion.

All their hopes lay in the fact that the town's team (called the Robins on a good day, and things unmentionable on a bad) was inconsistent. It seemed to every male inhabitant of the town, large and small, that most teams in the North-Eastern League knew their places in the League Table. Such grandees as Newcastle Reserves and Sunderland Reserves reigned in glory at the top, augmented thrillingly by ancient internationals recovering from a leg injury or a bad night on the beer and the manager's disfavour.

And the teams at the bottom, the Colliery Welfares, knew their place too, with their madly sloping pitches composed of cowpats and slag from the pit-heaps. But North Shields Robins could never make their mind up. They would shoot up the league table to third, inspiring the local paper to talk of appearing at Wembley. Then they would suddenly lose six games in a row, and plummet, and industrial production at the shipyards and guano-works would plummet with them, reducing the local reporters to wondering if Appleby Park shouldn't be sold up to build new houses on. And, when the team played badly, spectators walked out in disgust. Even before half-time. And left the gate swinging open for every small boy in the town to creep in. Whereas, if they were winning, the gate stayed tight shut right till the end.

'We should get in today,' said Sam. 'Blackhill are bottom of the league. And if we were to win, we'd go second too!' A broken staccato sound came winging over the chimneys. As of players being advised to knock the cowmuck off their boots, or get a set of crutches. Or go and decorate their wives' bedrooms.

'Blackhill's taken the field,' said Sam. They all nodded sagely. Then a happy roar. 'We've taken the field. And nobody's tripped over yet.' Then an acid storm of booing. 'The referee's come out.' And a groan. 'We lost the toss. Again.' They sat listening: and swaying in unison. A slow crescendo of joy. 'Charlie Blackstone. Dribbling down the right wing.

Good old Charlie.' A scream of rage. Followed by a loud whistle. 'They tripped him up, the dirty swine. Penalty.' But the following buzz wasn't loud enough. 'Only a free kick.' A deep groan followed. 'And he's put it wide.' Finally, after many minutes, a jubilant roar.

'One-nil,' said Billy. 'To Robins. We'll never get in today now.'

'Wait,' said Sam. 'You know them . . .' And he was right. Five minutes later, the sound of a huge animal dying in torment. 'Blackhill have equalised.' And soon, another dreadfully similar sound. 'Blackhill two, Robins one! Time to get moving, lads.' They hurried out, and up Hawkey's Lane. Halfway up, just after they had heard a third dreadful sound, they met a comfortably unbuttoned drunk. With a half-consumed froth-necked bottle in each pocket of his raincoat, and a football newspaper stuffed in each pocket of his sports coat. His tie was undone, and his trilby hat on the back of his head.

'Harry Mackintosh, of the *Shields Weekly News*,' said Sam, who was an expert. 'Off to write up the match. What's the headline this week, Harry?' The man bleared at them. 'Robins crash to rampant Blackhill,' he said. 'But I know what it should be: "Bring in the death penalty for Vince Albrother." He missed two open goals. I don't know how he managed to miss the second. He was only a foot out. My grannie coulda' done better.'

'Who does your grannie play for, Harry?' asked Sam.

'Glasgow Rangers, you little tyke!' Harry aimed a

blow at Sam's head, missed, and stayed upright by clinging to a lamppost.

The next man they met was tearing his football programme into little tiny pieces, and strewing them like confetti. Albert started to pick them up, but everyone told him there'd be better programmes on the ground further on. There were. Some not even crumpled. There was another dire groan from behind the high, tarry wall, with its rusted advertisements for Bovril and Andrews Liver Salts.

'Vince's missed an open goal again,' said Sam philosophically. A long whistle went.

'Half-time,' said Sam. Ahead men were leaving the gate in a steady stream, some pointing out lampposts convenient to hang Vince Albrother from. Quite a few men had a hand over their eyes, as at a graveside, and one was audibly weeping.

'You look forward to it all the week . . .'

'Mebbe there'll be tinned salmon for tea, George.'

'Aah couldn't eat a bite.' The gates were swinging open. They walked in. By this time they'd picked up about four perfectly unspoilt programmes each. Though what use they were . . . Still, they'd once cost threepence each.

'They don't give money back on them, do they?' asked Albert. They assured him not. 'But there's a raffle, Albert! The programme with the lucky number'll win!' It was a barefaced lie, but Albert began picking up every programme in sight.

It was a pleasant afternoon. The westering sun was shining on a green pitch, the cheery red jerseys of the Robins, and the incredibly cheap scruffy-looking mustard jerseys of Blackhill Colliery

Welfare. On the far side of the field the covered stand was in shadow, with a continuous flicker of flame as blokes lit up fags. The blokes in the stand, having paid more for their seats, were staying. But again Billy was lost in wonder that at every moment of the game, there was some bloke lighting up a fag. Maybe only when the Robins were losing . . .

There was a cripple on the touchline, offering Vince Albrother his crutches. There was a blind man, offering the referee his white stick and dark glasses. It must have had some effect. Vince Albrother fell down in the Blackhill goalmouth, and began writhing like a maggot in a bait tin.

'Foul,' yelled the remaining spectators, without hope. 'Penalty! Get your eyes checked, ref.' The referee blew his whistle very loud, to make up for blowing it very late. Vince Albrother took the penalty. Hit the crossbar with a terrible crack. The ball, by a miracle, rebounded to his feet. He kicked again, hit the crossbar another fearful smack. The rebound hit him in the chest this time, and trickled over the line for a goal.

'Goal,' shouted Sam, heroically, his small voice echoing around the ground in a lonely way.

'Not a proper goal,' said Nat. 'He frightened the goalie into surrendering. The goalie was lying on his face with his hands over his head.'

'Goal,' shouted Sam defiantly. He loved the Robins, and they gave him a lot of pain.

The Robins' third goal was even more ridiculous. The Blackhill forwards were hammering away at the Robins' end so hard that Sam had hidden his eyes down behind the billboards in his anguish. And the Blackhill goalie had drifted up the field to watch the fun. Except that the fun had been going on quite a long time, and the goalie had drifted a very long way from his goal. So when the Robins' goalie got his hands on the ball, and gave it the hugest possible kick to give himself some peace . . . The ball bounced. Clean over the Blackhill goalie's head. It then went on bouncing majestically down the field with the Blackhill goalie in hot pursuit. Ten yards out, he nearly caught up with it. Then he tripped, and fell on his face. The ball paused on the goal-line. As if suddenly nervous. And then a gust of wind blew it over. After that, Vince Albrother became like a man inspired. The final result was 4–3 to the Robins. And as the boys turned to go, they saw that, miraculously, the ground was full again. Not only had the original spectators returned, drawn by more hopeful sounds travelling across the warm air and the black chimney-pots. But there were also men who'd been out walking their dogs and families with little kids, and even housewives in carpet-slippers and their hair in curlers.

'Well done, Vince,' shouted one of them. 'You know where to put it, don't you?'

The Brylcreemed Vince gave her a lascivious grin and said, 'I'll be down for me supper, Ma.'

'And I'll give you a good hot one,' said the lady, not to be outfaced.

Meanwhile, Albert had picked up every programme in sight. He was carrying a pile of programmes so high, he could hardly see over the top of them. He had bundles stuffed in every pocket.

'One of them's *bound* to have the lucky number,' he said. 'I'm off to collect my winnings.' They watched him vanish up the wooden stairs of the club building.

'Poor swine,' said Henry. 'They gave up having a lucky number on the programme a year ago.'

'It kept him quiet. It kept him happy. So he didn't ask daft questions all the time.'

'He needs something to keep him occupied.'

'By gum, I'd like to be a fly on the wall in there. Bet he comes out flaming berserk.' But in the end Albert came out smiling, without the programmes. He held out a filthy hand, and showed them a worn threepenny bit.

'That's not a *prize*!' gasped Sam.

'No. He gave it to me for picking up all the litter. Says I've saved him half-an-hour. And his back's playing up something cruel today.'

The gang eyed the threepenny bit avidly.

'Chip-shop'll be open, Albert!'

'Bag o'chips all round, and *two* for you!'

Albert clenched his fist round the coin, as if he was going to argue.

'Picking up the programmes was our idea, Albert!' said Billy, asserting his authority. Albert eyed them, then nodded. It was four to one. Even he could count that much. On the way down town to the chip-shop, Sam said: 'Hey, I hope somebody phoned up Harry Mackintosh, and told him the final result!' But when they got out of the queue at the chip-shop, the paper-lads were already shouting around their Sporting Pinks: 'Robins crash to rampant Blackhill.'

'They'll sack him for sure now,' said Henry, worried.

'Garn. He does it all the time.' They had a good laugh. All but Billy. He walked along deep in thought. Vince Albrother, making all those mistakes, being hated by everybody. But keeping on trying. And winning in the end. Albert, picking up all those programmes for nowt, and then getting threepence out of nowhere. Albert, stupid though he was, had won too. He thought about certain school lessons. Aesop's fable about the tortoise and the hare. Robert the Bruce and the spider. He had always thought till now that all victories were well planned, glorious, a foregone conclusion. But that wasn't the way that victory had come to Albert, or Vince Albrother. Maybe you won just by going on. Staying hopeful. He took a deep breath and squared his shoulders. The Misses Crimond could be beaten yet.

CHAPTER 7

Fireworks

They were sitting in Sam's mam's wash-house, the next Saturday morning, staring out at the rain and comparing fireworks. Sam's dad had recently bought his mam, after years of scrimping and saving, that wonder of modern science, a wash-boiler. An upright cylinder on three legs, big as an oil-drum, its blue enamel speckled as a leopard's spots, or the stars in the night sky. On top was a shiny handle you revolved to and fro, that washed the clothes inside. Beneath, a real gas ring roared fiercely on the end of its flexible pipe and brought the water right to the boil, without any bother of lighting a fire. The wondrous thing was filled by a hose from the cold tap, where it stood in the kitchen corner.

Now, Sam's mam was free of carrying endless buckets of water and coal, of beating the clothes in the poss-tub with a poss-stick as big as a wooden cannon, of emptying the old poss-tub down the drain in the yard afterwards and wrenching her back. And, most blessed of all, she could wash on wet Mondays, when all the other mums, unable to poss in the backyard, fumed and fretted in idleness, with all the rest of their week – Tuesday ironing day, Wednesday cleaning day, Thursday baking day and Friday shopping day – set hopelessly out of joint.

What did it matter that now, every Monday, Sam's house filled with steam, the windows ran rivers, and the wallpaper on the staircase bulged with great damp-blisters and Sam's family had to eat their dinner in a tropical rainforest atmosphere? Such was the price that had to be paid for progress and the bottomless envy and admiration of the neighbours . . .

But the immeasurable boon for the lads was that they now had a place to meet on wet days. The wash-house, with its boiler, furnace and chimney, was now the haunt only of spiders and the Wash-house Club. By hook or by crook, the gang had gathered three-legged stools and crackets and chopping-blocks to sit on. And Sam had draped sacking each side of the window, in a way that still let light in, but stopped Sam's mam's prying eyes. An old bolt on the inside of the door, and they were as snug as a bug in a rug. When Sam's mam was out, they could even pinch paper and sticks and coal and get a fire going and roast stolen potatoes; lovely, teeth-screechingly raw within, but their outsides blackened to charcoal.

But no fire today. Today they were comparing fireworks. Fireworks began appearing in the windows of the corner shops at the end of September. They bought them one by one as money cropped up, whether windfalls from rich relatives visiting, or empty lemonade bottles snitched and taken back to the shop for a ha'penny. It took so long to choose which firework to buy! Two Catherine wheels for a penny, or a glorious fat Roman candle. Six volcanoes for threepence, or the wild glory of a threepenny rocket that would explode on the night so that the whole town would notice. Or three packets of sparklers to wave round your head in a wild dance with your mates. Or, loveliest of all, jumping jacks to throw at crowds of girls on Guy Fawkes' Night in the hope that one would leap up their knickers. Jumping jacks were such insignificant things – a tube of white paper wrapped in a tight zigzag. They made no flash or lovely fountain of sparks, but they had minds of their own like cats. If a girl ran away, a jumping jack might pursue her to her very doorstep. Then lie silent, as if dead. Until she turned back, ashamed of her fear, and then it would leap out of hiding and be after her knickers again . . . bang, leap, bang, leap. Oh, such *delicious* screaming.

Or, one could go in for madness, and blue a whole sixpence on a rocket with a three-foot stick, like Nat was holding up now, and dusting off lovingly with his handkerchief and stroking like a pet dog. 'Waste o' money,' sniffed Albert Snowdon. He was poorest of all with just five ha'penny wonders. He had been known to hover, staring into the shop window for an hour, mumbling and shifting from foot to foot in his anxiety whether to choose a snow shower or a daisy fountain. And since, once set alight, they both looked exactly alike . . .

They had done well for fireworks this year. They

sat amidst an abundance of purple cones and squat trench mortars. Their guy had done well, down the town. It had been a brainwave of Billy's, like only Billy could have, that kept him, in spite of all disasters, the leader of the gang.

They had had no trouble getting a bogie. That vehicle made of a massive plank with four pram wheels that was essential transport for any guy. Henry had a beauty. The wheels were huge. They had come from his married sister's pram, a very splendid carriage. Henry's sister had had such sufferings with her first-born that she had sworn to have no more, and had given the pram to Henry in a fit of pique after a row with her husband, who wanted four children. By the time the baby-loving husband returned home from work, the gorgeous but now wheel-less carriage was sinking in the mud of Lolly's Pond, and Henry had a fine new bogie. Henry's sister had a black eye for two weeks after, but Henry reckoned it was well worth it. The pram had been second-hand or third-hand anyway . . .

To make the guy they had had a whip-round, ha'penny each (except Albert who was broke as usual), and bought a Guy Fawkes' mask, all yellow and evil with eye-slits and a big black curling moustache. They took Henry's dad's fishing hat with the long pheasant's feather (fishing was out of season); a good tweed overcoat Billy had outgrown, and which just hung in the cupboard because he had no smaller brothers and sisters; a pair of Sam's dad's dungarees with a hole in the knee, and Albert's only pair of wellies (sacrifices had to be made for the good of all, though they had to twist his ear;) a pair of Nat's mam's kid gloves (they were summer gloves and she wouldn't miss them.) Besides, she'd get them back *eventually*: this was a guy for making money, not for burning.

They had all the outsides; the trouble was the insides. They could never get them right. Stuffing the coat and dungarees with straw and tying them together was bad enough. But attaching the head and wellies . . . they always drooped and flopped and fell off at the most embarrassing money-making moment, and grown-ups who'd been about to cough up a penny, who even had taken a penny out of their pockets, put it back saying they'd give it next year, when poor Guy came out of hospital, if he lived that long, har-har.

'Oh, the *insides*,' groaned Nat.

'Got an idea,' said Billy.

'What?'

Billy kicked Albert, where he lay drooped against the wall, dozing, mouth open, in the bright autumn sun coming through the wash-house window.

'*He* can be the guy. He's half-dead already. He won't feel a thing.'

Albert protested. In vain. In face of threats of exclusion from the gang for ever, he allowed himself to be dressed up, and strapped to the bogie with many strands of old rope. He made a splendid guy: his neck didn't droop, at least not unrealistically. And the wellies, being his own, did not fall off.

'Better-looking than he used to be,' said Nat, adjusting the mask.

'Quite handsome. His own mother wouldn't recognise him.'

'I've got *another* idea,' announced Billy.

'What?' they cried in amazed admiration.

'If we attached some strings to his belt, when we tugged them, he could move his head and arms. Like a puppet. Everyone would be amazed.'

Albert objected, but they just gave him the odd kick or two. Not cruel. Just like you might whip up a lazy horse. It worked splendidly. They tugged the strings; his head wagged from side to side, his arms rose and fell. It was most realistic.

'We gotta get a good site to display him.'

'Outside Woolworths' is best.'

'The Stevensons have their guy there. Every year.'

'Not if we get there first.'

'How can we get there first? You can't hurry Albert.'

'I'll go to the Stevenson's house Saturday morning. Offer to sell them cut-price fireworks. Say me mam is on her death-bed and I need the money for medicine,' said Sam. Sam too was acknowledged a genius. *If* he could hold up the Stevensons for half an hour. So on Saturday morning, Billy and Nat and Henry set off, pulling Albert on the bogie.

Albert said, 'Ow, me bum,' every time they went over a kerb too fast, but there were no other accidents. For once, the guy's head stayed on. And the site outside Woolworths' was still vacant . . . Good old scheming Sam. This was worth losing a bit of money on, selling fireworks to the Stevensons.

The town, or rather that part of town which was grown up and had pennies to spare, was amazed. Henry pulled the strings which led to Albert's belt, and Albert duly wagged his head and raised his arms. Nobody had seen anything like it. Pennies just rained into the old cap at Albert's feet. Even the policeman gave them a ha'penny and, for once, did not move them on.

There was a nasty moment when Albert, getting carried away with his role, suddenly uttered, from the mouth of the mask, the words, 'Fee, fi, fo, fum!' The old lady whose hand had been poised over the cap with two pennies, suddenly dropped them and they went rolling into the gutter. Nat dived and snaffled them in time.

Billy, pointing to Henry, said, thereby saving the day: 'It's all right, madam. This boy is a gifted ventriloquist. He is going on the stage with it, when he grows up.'

'Eeh, Aah nearly had a heart attack,' said the lady. 'You can have too much of a good thing . . .' She departed, still clutching the place where she thought her heart was which, as Billy pointed out, was on the wrong side.

'You hear that, Guy Fawkes?' said Nat savagely. 'Too much of a good thing. D'you want to get us *arrested*?' He looked nervously at the policeman, who was still watching them from a way off, giving appreciative smiles from time to time. Guy Fawkes subsided with a hollow groan.

Then the Stevensons turned up with their guy, which looked very ordinary by comparison, and whose head did immediately fall off the moment his bogie stopped.

'*Our* place,' said the biggest Stevenson, dangerously. 'Hop it.'

'That policeman's our mate,' said Billy stoutly.

'He gave us a whole penny.'

'Our place,' said Big Stevenson, taking Billy by the throat.

'Help, police!' called out Billy, falsetto. 'Murder.'

'He's coming over,' said one of the smaller Stevensons, nervously.

'Now then,' said the constable, looming.

The Stevensons took to their heels, the eldest muttering to Billy, 'Wait till I get you at school, Monday morning.'

After that, it was all peace and money. Until Albert suddenly announced: 'Aah want to go to the lavvy.'

'Cross your legs,' said Nat savagely.

'Whoever saw a guy with crossed legs?' asked Henry.

'We'll have to take him.'

'How?'

'Carry him. If we move the bogie, Stevensons will come back and nick our place,' said Henry. 'I'll stay wi' bogie.'

It was perhaps a mistake to try to carry him through Woolworths'. Though Nat said it was a short cut. They got a lot of stares. But it was when Albert forgot himself so far as to reach up and scratch his nose . . .

A woman screamed and fainted.

Nat and Billy dropped Albert. All three took to their heels. Albert's mask got twisted, blinding him. He took a wrong turning up a side aisle, and his head popped up suddenly from behind one of the counters next to an assistant serving crystallised fruits . . .

Another woman fainted.

But they all reached the Wash-house Club safely in the end. Including good old Henry, his pockets so full of pennies he could hardly walk.

Yes, they had a lot of fireworks that year. Except poor Albert, who hadn't the sense to hide his share of the loot, and was forced to spend it buying a birthday present for his hated sister.

'Maybe,' said Billy dreamily, 'we could use our fireworks against Miss Crimond.'

'You mean,' gasped Nat, 'fire rockets at her windows?'

'A Roman candle through the letterbox?' asked Henry.

'I do not,' said Billy in a lordly voice, 'wish to end up in the police court.'

'How then?'

'We once put a banger inside a tomato through Mr Miller's letterbox,' said Sam, with a happy reminiscent smile. 'And we once put a banger inside a bunch of flowers on Granny Moore's doorstep, knocked and ran away. It went up like confetti, just as she was reaching down saying, "Ooh, how lovely!"'

'No,' said Billy. 'That was just fun. This is serious.'

'What then?'

'Jumping jacks. Hundreds of jumping jacks. Into their back yard, in through their letterbox. All together.

'We've only got half a dozen,' objected Nat. 'And we're broke.'

'The man at the corner shop might change the fireworks we've got already,' said Billy. They all looked at him in horror. Nat cuddled his sixpenny rocket. Sam gathered his six big fat Roman candles to his bosom, as if they were his own flesh and blood. They had lived with those fireworks, adored them, laid them out and counted them on the hearthrug of an evening for weeks. They were like members of the family . . . some of them even had special names. It wouldn't even be worth collecting stuff for a bonfire without them. A miserable Guy Fawkes' Night, wandering around hoping to get a glimpse of other people's . . .

'It's a case of national sacrifice,' said Billy finally. 'There'll be other Guy Fawkes's . . . Maybe if the Misses Crimond were gone, we could have our big bonfire in the front street . . .'

He got up slowly, having made his point, and picked up great fat Vesuvius, three inches across its base. And his flaming onions and Versailles fountain. One by one, slowly, silently, reluctantly, they followed him, bearing those they had loved, and were about to lose for ever.

The shopman picked up fat Vesuvius, turned it upside-down to inspect the base, undid the blue touch-paper and sniffed inside as if it were a scent bottle.

'You've not set it off,' he said, still looking for the snag. 'Nor dropped it in the water. I know it's not last year's 'cos I sold it to you and we didn't have none of these last year . . . what're you selling it for?'

'We need jumping jacks,' said Billy stolidly. 'Lots of jumping jacks.'

'You must know lots of girls,' said the man.

'Two girls in particular,' said Billy, in his meaningful voice. The shopman looked across the road, at the Misses Crimond's house; his face turned a bit more friendly. He had had his own troubles with the Misses Crimond. They had accused him several times of selling single cigarettes to children; and complained to the Weights and Measures about his scales, which had given him a very nasty turn one Saturday morning when he was rushed off his feet. Then he took Nat's sixpenny rocket from Nat's nerveless hand.

'I only sold this to you two days ago. I can't give you the full price back, you know. I've got to have me profit and me overheads. I'll give you six jumping jacks for it.

Nat turned pale and clenched his teeth. 'Eight,' he said. Jumping Jacks were only a ha'penny.

'Seven,' said the shopman, and passed them over. 'Lucky I got plenty left. Whereas you can't get these rockets now, so close to Guy Fawkes', for love nor money.'

Silently, one by one, they handed over their best friends, and stuffed their pockets with the crimped concertinas of white paper.

'This had better work,' said Nat.

'You'll be needing fuses,' said the shopman. 'To light them with, quick. One after the other. No time for matches . . .' And he held out five long bits of what looked like thick dark patterned string.

'We can't pay you,' said Billy.

'Have these on me,' said the shopman, with feeling. 'What time does the balloon go up?'

They decided on Guy Fawkes' Night itself: as soon as it was dark. Before the cats and dogs were called home and the night really started. They wouldn't have dared do it any other night but Guy Fawkes'. Any other night they would be arrested for sure. But on Guy Fawkes', the police seemed to think that boys would be boys . . .

'Sam and Henry in the front garden, for the letterbox,' said Billy. 'They're small, the hedge and gate will hide them, if they kneel down . . .'

'No,' said Sam.

'What d'you mean, no?' Billy's fist clenched at such insubordination when they were poised to Go Over The Top.

'I'm going on the roofs,' said Sam. 'I'm putting some down their chimney. That should settle it. I can get up our drainpipe. Me mam'll be out, and me dad not home from work.'

'Hey, steady on,' said Billy.

'Just 'cos you would be scared to do it . . .' Of course, that finished the argument, dead.

'All right,' said Billy grudgingly. 'Henry and Albert in the front garden. Albert can hold the letterbox open.' Even Albert couldn't mess up holding the letterbox open. Billy and Nat went in next-door's yard, which belonged to Nat's family. They would lie hidden on the coalhouse roof.

'Wait for my secret whistle,' said Billy.

'Don't try that whistling stuff,' said Henry. 'Just yell "Charge" or something. You can't whistle for toffee, and we'd never hear out front.'

'There's Sam now,' whispered Nat, as he lay on the slates of the coalhouse. 'Just behind the second chimney stack. I saw him light up his fuse with a match. You can see it glowing.' It looked like a tiny red firefly, up by the great black chimney. Billy had never realised that chimney-pots were so big, or Sam so small. He blew on his own fuse. It glowed yellow, then went dull red again. Was this how they had felt on the Western Front, when zero-hour came, and the whistles blew? Well . . .

'Charge,' he shouted. Nat lit his first jumping jack, checked it was burning strongly, and threw it into Crimonds' yard. It landed on Crimonds' windowsill, throwing off sparks. Billy hoped the impact hadn't put it out. Then it was light, throw, light, throw. They went so quick, his pockets were nearly empty when the first one went off. God, what a din! They lay, pressing their hands over their ears. Every time one went off, there was a flick of sparks and torn white paper. The whole yard was a sea of tiny jumping white shadows. People ran out of their houses, demanding to know what it was, where it was? But nothing was visible. It was all in the yard and the house. And in that warren of narrow yards, it could have come from anywhere.

One veteran said, 'Eeh, that put me in mind of the first battle of Mons. We shot so fast and hard that day, the Germans thought we all had machine-guns. We showed Kaiser Bill whether we were a contemptible little army or not.'

Another voice said, 'Oh, Dad, give over. Not that

old story again.' Then silence. Except that, high on the skyline of the roof, something was going wrong with Sam. Sam's jumping jacks were no longer going down the Misses Crimond's chimney. From what could be seen, they were leaping from his pockets and exploding all over the roof. Wailing with terror, the tiny black figure scampered along the ridge tiles pursued by a horde of small avenging white demons.

'Lord love me,' said one woman. 'What is it? The Return of Spring-heeled Jack?'

'Mebbe it's an advertising stunt for Brock's fireworks,' said her friend. By the time the little black figure had vanished with a long slide down the roof, which, after a heart-stopping pause, was not followed by the thud of a body on the ground, people were turning away saying, 'I think the circus must be in town. I never heard they were coming.'

'It's just boys being boys, I reckon. It *is* Guy Fawkes' Night.

Silence. Silence in street and back lane, silence in yards. Silence in the Misses Crimond's house. Only their dim gaslight glowed on the drawn blind.

Nat stretched, and said, in an interested voice: 'Mebbe they're dead. Mebbe they both had heart attacks and died.'

A horror of the condemned cell, and the noose, descended on Billy. It had been his idea. A scrabbling of steel toecaps warned of the arrival of Henry and Albert. They flung themselves down, panting.

'Any sign of them?'

'No sign,' said Billy, choking. More scrabbling announced the arrival of Sam.

'What happened to *you*?' they hissed.

'One hit the edge of the chimney pot and jumped back into my pocket. It set all the rest on fire. I haven't got any pocket left. Me mam'll skin me . . .' But eventually, he fell silent at the greater horror of the silent Crimond house.

'Perhaps they've just fainted,' said Henry hopefully. Nobody answered. And then . . . the sound of two sets of footsteps approaching. And a cutting female voice saying: 'I told her straight. I'm not paying one and elevenpence three farthings for those, I said. Not long ago, you could get real silk for that price.'

'Miss Crimond,' muttered Billy wrathfully, hiding all the relief that was flooding into his heart.

'So I made her put them back, and got a pair of thick lisle ones instead. Much more sensible for the winter.'

The Misses Crimond entered their back gate, only feet away from five sets of tight-sealed lips, five sets of held breath.

'Oh, look at the state of the yard. All those little bits of white paper, like confetti. Who's done that?'

'I'll sweep it tomorrow.'

'See you do.' They opened their back door. The voices grew fainter, but still audible.

'Oh, we've had a fall of soot. The hearth's full. Lucky we had the fireguard up.'

'Place'll need a good dusting . . .'

'Yes, but we've saved the cost of the sweep. Once we've dusted, we're half-a-crown to the good.'

'The front hall's full of that white confetti stuff too.'

'Whatever can have been happening? Well, it's an ill wind . . .'

'My lovely rocket,' gritted Nat. 'The best rocket I ever had. And what do we manage to do? Save them half-a-crown for the chimney-sweep. Next time I want *your* advice, Billy Leggett, I'll ask for it.'

There were subdued rebellious murmurs from all the gang as they climbed stiffly down. But it was better than the shadow of the hangman's noose.

There was more bad news when Billy got home.

'Your Cousin Emily's passed away,' said Mam. 'But I expect it was a blessed release.' She only sounded a bit upset: not like it was the end of the world. Cousin Emily had been unbelievably ancient.

But it meant a funeral, and Billy did not much like funerals.

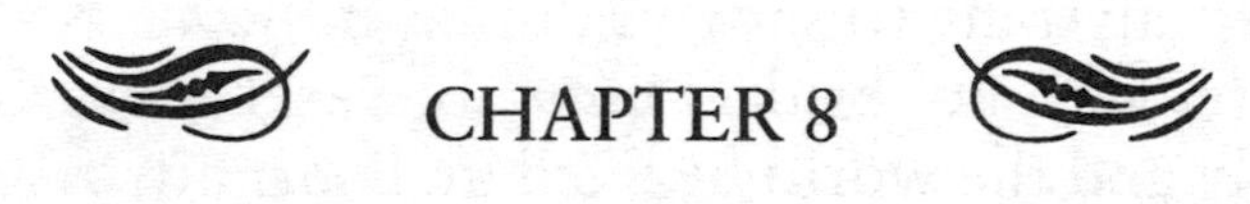

CHAPTER 8

Cousin Emily

The death of Cousin Emily affected Billy strangely. For one thing, she had never seemed really alive. Ever since he could remember, she had been in bed in the big upstairs bedroom at Lovaine Place, a tiny wizened apple of a face and faded blue eyes peeping out of a mass of frills and lace, mob-cap, pillows, sheets. The most alive thing about Cousin Emily had been her smell – she smelt of wintergreen and eucalyptus, friar's balsam and mentholated whatsits – the smell rolled downstairs like an avalanche as soon as Cousin Annie, Emily's daughter, opened the front door.

Cousin Annie now, *she* was alive. Plump and strong and bouncing in her brown dress and white apron, like a female blackbird. Full of enquiries about everyone's health and well-being, ready hands offering ginger wine, amazing biscuits, cups of cocoa and enormous boxes of chocolates. But nothing was sweeter than her big, anxious, loving brown eyes. She was a favourite of Billy's, with her stories about the Great War, and the exploits of her hero, Sir John French. Billy might have gone to her house much more often, had it not been that sooner or later, you had to mount the deep-carpeted stairs to see Cousin Emily, in her rich mentholated tomb, where she lay in state like a female Pharaoh in all her splendour. He never stayed long, for there was never anything to say: all thoughts died in his head. There was no bridge crossable, between Cousin Emily and the world he lived in. But it always ended with plunging forward recklessly through the cloud of eucalyptus, thick as chlorine gas on the Western Front in the Great War, and with no hope of a gas mask. And seeing the straggling hairs on her chin, and hearing her false teeth give a tiny click as you kissed her. She would grope for your hand with her little tiny claw, with the slowness of an insect, and press into your hand a shiny shilling, scarcely warmed by her flesh, however long she had held it in waiting. Then, downstairs, pell-mell and out through the open front door into the sunlit garden, to breathe for the first time in five minutes; the rich smells of roses and purple heliotrope, yellow mignonette and the even richer smell of the horse manure Cousin Emily's gardener put on her roses.

And now, it would never happen again, because Cousin Emily was dead. And in the cold ground, and perhaps there would be no more shillings. And they were back at Cousin Emily's, which you must now call Cousin Annie's, for the funeral tea. Dying for a glimpse of the roaring fire, because the view of it was entirely blocked by the giant bodies of Uncle Horace and Uncle George, lifting up their jacket-tails to warm their black-suited bums, and discussing how trade was.

'I never accept less than three per cent interest on

my investments,' said Uncle Horace. 'No matter how hard the times.'

'True, true,' said Uncle George, shaking his head. He was the lesser, and knew it: three years younger, his head less shiningly bald, his waistcoat less formidably bulging, his gold watch-chain a little thinner, and the red precious stone that hung in his fob a little smaller.

'People must be prepared to make sacrifices,' said Uncle George.

'*Which* people?' snapped Uncle Horace, so that even Uncle George quailed slightly and said hurriedly: 'The workers. The workers, of course. These ridiculous demands they're making . . .'

'*Ridiculous*!' Uncle Horace stopped him dead, as if he had shot him with an elephant rifle. But now a new voice joined in from across the room.

'What's that about the workers?' Uncle Stan was already in disgrace. For one thing, he was not a *real* uncle, so it was not his place to speak. Merely a very old friend of Cousin Emily's. For another thing, he had turned up for the funeral rather wobbly on his feet and smelling of whisky. He had talked of Cousin Emily in a loud voice, as if she were not merely still alive, but about eighteen years old.

'Prettiest little dancer I ever did see. Nobody could waltz like Emily. She would dance the whole night away . . .' He began to pom-pom the tune of 'The Blue Danube', beating time in the air with his arm, and almost knocking an ornament off the mantelpiece. Eventually, the surrounding silence of disapproval grew so cold, the tuttings and glances so marked that even Uncle Stan subsided with a last cry of 'Those were the days. The good old days.' Leaving everyone to stare at his raincoat and brown boots. *Brown* boots at a funeral indeed! Nobody spoke to him at all.

But he and Billy had exchanged sympathetic looks. For not only was this revelation that Aunt Emily had not spent her whole life in bed truly amazing, but it seemed to him that Uncle Stan was the only one who showed any love for her at all. Nobody else had even spoken her name. They had even tutted Uncle Stan into silence when he started to cry. But then, what more was to be expected? He had squandered all the money his father had left him on drink and women; he had ended up a bricklayer's labourer and boasted proudly of it. Above all, he had read all the works of Lenin and Marx, and spouted them on every available occasion, drunk or sober.

'How's your property down by the river doing?' asked Uncle Horace.

Uncle George pulled a face. 'The cost of repairs! You can charge the tenants for a broken window, but you can't charge when the wind blows slates off the roof. Property's a nightmare under the present government.'

'All property is *theft*,' shouted Uncle Stan loudly. 'Lenin said so in 1917.'

'You can say that again, Stan,' said Dad, who had been unavailingly trying to get nearer the fire to warm his own backside, but had been beaten back by vigorous shoves of Uncle Horace's.

'Now, now, you men,' said Cousin Annie,

bustling in. 'Here's my poor mother scarcely cold in her grave, and you men quarrelling about politics. You ought to have more respect for the dead.'

'Lenin's dead,' said Uncle Stan. 'Marx and Engles are dead too. That's why we should have respect for them.'

'Hush, you,' said Cousin Annie, not without affection. 'Take a salmon sandwich. Let your meat stop your mouth.'

'Those two would steal bread from the mouths of babes,' said Uncle Stan, through a spray of salmon crumbs. 'They never stop grinding the faces of the workers. They say Horace pays the lowest wages of any ship sailing out of the Tyne. So low, only the heathen Chinese will sail for him, 'cos they don't understand our money. Ah well, wait till the revolution comes.'

'Mebbe we women'll see a bit of the fire when the revolution comes,' said Aunt Nellie, who was Uncle George's wife, and who never dared stand up to him except in company at funerals after her second sherry.

'So what would Lenin call my uncles?' Billy asked Uncle Stan with great interest. Uncle Stan nearly went cross-eyed, between eating his next salmon sandwich, and this delightful question.

'*Rentiers*, Marx would'a called them.' Billy must have looked disappointed.

'Capitalist profiteers.' Uncle Stan tried again. That was a bit better.

'Vultures, hyenas, running dogs of capitalist society. Adventurists . . .' Uncle Stan's voice had gone up to a bellow. 'When Trotsky and the Red Army get here, they'll be strung up from the nearest lamp-post.'

'They'll need very strong lamp-posts,' said Billy, awed.

'We're just going for a breath of air, Annie,' said Uncle Horace in a very huffy voice. 'If you can fetch us our coats. We'll not be long.' They stood, lordly, while poor Cousin Annie, laden with garments, heaved their coats onto their bodies, while they just stood and let her. When the door slammed behind them, there was a sigh of relief, and a general movement towards the fire. Now Dad and the Vicar were standing there warming their bums, but since both were as thin as rails, plenty of flame was cheerfully visible to everyone in the room.

Moreover, released from the weight of Horace and George's business worries, appetites revived. Second cups of tea, another queen cake, even a little sip of whisky were indulged in. All kinds of topics were spoken of. The vicar admitted with a beam that the organ fund was doing well; ladies fell to talk of knitting patterns and Fair Isle jumpers, whooping cough and women's burdens, which men would never understand. Dad was heard discussing football teams for once, and the curate briefly described his cycling tour of the English Riviera. The only topic never mentioned was Cousin Emily, though Billy had strange broken visions of her rising from her death-bed and waltzing round the room to the sound of 'The Blue Danube'. To empty his mind of such visions, he put the case of the Misses Crimond to Uncle Stan. Uncle Stan nodded gravely.

'Grinding the faces of the poor right enough,' he opined. 'Fancy! Inspecting the insides of homes like that, every Friday! Even Lenin would admit that an Englishman's home is his castle. Yes, lad, you're right in the front line of the struggle of the proletariat. Workers of the world unite! You have nothing to lose but your chains . . .'

It seemed to Billy quite wonderful that a man as great and famous as Lenin should have turned his mind to the affairs of Back Tennyson Street.

CHAPTER 9

The Plan

'We could try the privies,' said Sam, after long thought. The plan of campaign against Miss Crimond was continuing.

The whole gang brightened a bit. There was good fun in privies. They were at the bottom of people's yards, as far away from the houses as possible, because they were nothing like flush toilets and made an awful smell, especially in summer, and even more especially if the Midnight Mechanics were slow in coming to empty the big smelly buckets, which they did through a special hatch into the back lane.

But in winter, after dark, you could creep silently along the row of privy hatches, and shine your torch in, looking for the twin pale pendulous half-moons that meant someone was sitting on the seat above, all innocent of your presence. Then you could give them the fright of their lives by howling like a banshee. Or if you had a can of cold water, or in winter a snowball . . .

But that was just a joke all kids played, even on people you quite liked, like Mr Miller's family. It wasn't *serious*.

‘Kid’s stuff,’ said Billy contemptuously.

‘Our next-door neighbours’ tom-cat,’ mused Sam, ‘he’s quite friendly. He’ll come if you call him, specially if you’ve got a bit of bacon rind. We could put him in a sack, and give him a poke to make him good an’ mad, and then if we put *him* in their privy . . .’

Everybody laughed like a drain. ‘C’mon, let’s,’ said Nat.

‘It’s quite a good plan,’ said Billy loftily. ‘But I think I can make it better. Give me a chance to think about it.’

‘Big ’ead,’ said Sam.

Oddly, inspiration came to Billy when he was sitting on his own privy, last thing one night.

He’d lit the candle in the jamjar, wrapped its string round his wrist and ventured down the cold dark rainy yard before bed. It was quite snug inside, with the door bolted and the candlelight flickering on the walls. Of course there was the peep-hole in the privy door, that Count Dracula might be looking through at this very moment . . . but he was inclined to think the good Count had better things to do with his time than visit Back Tennyson Street.

It was then the plan came to him. Mrs Vicar, the innocent Vicar’s even more innocent wife. She always came to see Mam on Thursday nights, because they were both in the Garments for the Poor Knitting Circle. The Garments for the Poor was a disaster, because all the parish ladies who could really knit were busy knitting for their own families. It was those who couldn’t knit, whose families refused to wear their ghastly knitting, who inflicted it on the poor. And every Thursday night, Mrs Vicar came round to Mam with a bag of dreadful garments, wavery-edged scarves, pairs of socks of which one was twice the size of the other, balaclava helmets that would not fit a shrunken head from Borneo headhunters . . . unless Mrs Vicar and Mam did something to improve them. They called this 'making up' the garments. Dad said they made them up like some people made up lies and fairy-tales . . .

Mrs Vicar was fond of Billy. She liked him to sit at her feet on the clippie hearthrug while she told him stories about the boy Jesus. This had certain disadvantages, since there was really only one story about the boy Jesus, and the ones Mrs Vicar made up were pretty unbelievable. Also, when he had to sit on the hearthrug he could not help seeing up her knickers, which as she was pretty plump was no great treat, making him feel he was being wicked without any kind of profit such as might have come from looking up somebody younger's knickers . . .

But she was a sweet loving gentle soul, and really he was quite fond of her, so he did his duty so as not to hurt her feelings. If it was raining outside and there was nowt else to do, anyway.

The plan leapt to his mind in a flash. The only thing was, Sam must remember to say Billy's name . . .

It was cosy by the fire in the range. Outside, the wind howled in the blackness, and threw sharp volleys of rain against the pink-curtained windows.

Mam was busy unravelling back the sleeves of a jumper that would have fitted an orang-utan with knuckles trailing on the ground.

Mrs Vicar snapped a piece of wool between her nice white teeth and said, 'The boy Jesus must have been a shepherd, because later he was always talking about sheep. And he talked about wolves, ravening wolves, too. So he must have faced up to a ravening wolf when he was still quite small . . .'

Billy felt very safe; as safe as if he had been sitting at the feet of God Himself, so great was his respectability tonight. But the ravening wolves were prowling outside in the dark and rain. Nat and Henry with the tom-cat in its sack; they'd kept it without food for twelve hours in Henry's mam's wash-house, and given it the occasional poke through the sack to hear its reassuring snarls. It had even clawed Henry's hand and drawn blood, right through the sack.

Wolves approaching Miss Crimond's privy.

Across the hearth, Dad sucked on a dry pipe miserably and read the Sunday paper again, since they could no longer afford a daily one.

It was a long, long time, almost for ever, before the female scream finally resounded down the back lane.

'Dear Lord, what's that?' Mrs Vicar clutched her throat nervously. 'Some poor soul being murdered . . .'

'Drunks more likely,' said Dad, without taking his head out of the paper. He was in a bad mood tonight, with no tobacco and no new paper, and he couldn't even show it, because Mrs Vicar was present.

'Go and see, William,' said Mam severely. They must not seem uncaring in front of Mrs Vicar.

Grumbling softly to himself, Dad put down the paper and went down the yard, and then came back wiping the rain off his sleeves, saying, 'Nowt. Not a soul in sight. Drunks, I told you.'

Everyone settled back round the fire. 'And just imagine,' continued Mrs Vicar, 'that small child facing a rabid, ravening *wolf*. But perhaps he had a sling to defend himself with, like the boy David . . .'

Only Billy knew how near the rabid ravening wolf was approaching. He huddled closer to Mrs Vicar, his sole true protector, listening for enraged footsteps, his lips sealed, but his heart pounding.

There came a thunderous knocking on the front door.

'More drunks,' said Dad wearily.

'Go and sort them out, William.'

He sighed, got up again. Billy heard his soft slippered tread up the front passage.

Then a cold gale blew in, making the living-room door swing wide. The front door banged open to the wall, he heard Dad say, 'What the . . .?'

And then Miss Crimond was in the room, looking twice her normal size with rage. And just behind her, looking even more huge in his rain-shiny cape and pointed helmet, a policeman.

'That's him,' shouted Miss Crimond, and leaning over Mrs Vicar very rudely, she snatched Billy to his feet with both hands.

She picked him off the ground by both shoulders, and shook him till his teeth rattled.

'You little . . . *savage*! You little *criminal*! You

filthy little *guttersnipe*! Arrest him, constable!' She threw Billy from her, so he fell into the hearth, setting the poker and tongs flying in all directions with a terrifying crash. Billy's head hit the fender with an agonising bang. He couldn't speak for the pain, which was perhaps just as well.

Mam picked him up, and clutched him to her bosom, glaring at Miss Crimond like a tigress defending her young to the death.

'Steady on, ladies,' said the constable with great but uneasy authority. Fights between grown females, though rare, were always the worst to break up; embarrassing too . . . 'Now, let's view this calmly . . .'

'This . . . woman . . .' said Dad, in a voice of wrath, 'breaks into my house and nigh half-murders my son, and you expect me to view it calmly?'

'You must be *mad*!' said Mam, still glaring daggers at Miss Crimond.

'There have been allegations made,' said the constable, still trying to get a grip. 'An investigation is in progress . . .'

'What allegations?' roared Dad.

'The woman's mad,' said Mam again. 'Bursting into my house like that.'

'It has been alleged,' said the constable heavily, 'that a cat was put through the hatch into a privy . . . causing . . . actual bodily harm . . .' Now that nobody was actually assaulting each other, he seemed to be having great difficulty with his face.

A look of comprehension dawned on Dad's face. 'When was this?'

'About ten minutes ago, sir. At number one Back

Tennyson Street – in the back premises.'

'We heard a scream,' said Dad, as if wanting to be fair.

Miss Crimond drew herself up to her full quivering height, and said in awful tones, '*He* was the one who did it. I distinctly heard the other boy whisper "Here's the cat, Billy". And I've no doubt he's also the one behind the horse manure and the coal . . .'

The constable looked at Billy. An awful *arresting* sort of look. Billy could almost hear the handcuffs chinking in the pocket of his trousers . . .

It was here that the good Mrs Vicar, who had never been known to tell a lie, who could never have even been suspected of telling a lie, played the role appointed to her. She rose to her feet and, hand clutched to her throat, said, 'How dare you accuse this poor innocent little child? He has been sitting at my feet this last hour, listening to stories of the boy Jesus.'

It was alleged afterwards by Dad that Miss Crimond at this point told Mrs Vicar under her breath just where she ought to place the boy Jesus. That was what Dad told the street over the coming days, but he may just have been embroidering an already good story to avid listeners.

Certainly Mrs Vicar turned very pale, though she said nothing more, just placed a plump white hand protectively on Billy's shoulder.

'Is this true, madam?' There was a subtle change in the constable's voice that boded no good for Miss Crimond.

'Of course it's true,' said Mrs Vicar, outraged.

And Mam and Dad nodded vigorously. Billy thought Miss Crimond was going to blow a gasket. But she still yelled, 'Why did the other boy say "Billy" then?'

'World's full of Billies,' said Dad ominously. 'There's three Billies in the next street, to my knowledge. Billy Newton, Billy Smart and Billy Lattimer. And I wouldn't trust any of the little tykes as far as I could throw them.' His eye caught sight of the brass shovel still lying in the fireplace. It was very badly bent. How was anyone to know it was very old and bent very easily? Dad picked it up thoughtfully and tried to straighten it, and failed.

'I shall not be bringing any charges,' said the constable, starting to back towards the door uneasily. Miss Crimond looked as if she expected the ground to open up and swallow her.

'No charges, eh?' asked Dad slowly, a little cruelly. 'What about people bursting into my house without a by-your-leave, or people beating up my son when he'd done nowt? What about people ruinin' ma good shovel?'

Mam tenderly felt the back of Billy's head. 'There's a lump coming up the size of a hen's egg. And the skin's broken. He's *bleeding*.' She held up a bloodstained hand dramatically.

The constable coughed expectantly, and looked at Miss Crimond. He had no intention of charging a lady who was a pillar of society; more than his job was worth. But there was a way out of such matters . . .

'I shall pay you for the shovel,' said Miss Crimond, reaching into her coat pocket. 'Of course.

Two shillings should be sufficient.'

'That was my father's shovel,' said Dad. 'That shovel came from Preston Park. It's a family heirloom, not some of your Woolworths' rubbish. And what about my lad's head?'

Miss Crimond made a noise of disgust deep in her throat. Then reached in her purse and pulled out a gold sovereign and thumped it into Dad's hand.

'I'm sure that will cover any damage.' Then she stalked out, slamming the door behind her.

'I'll wish you goodnight, sir!' said the policeman, in a voice of deep thankfulness.

'A cup of tea, constable?' asked Mam, ever gracious.

'With a spot of something in it for the rain?' suggested Dad.

'Thank you, no, sir. I've had enough excitement for one evening. I have to meet my sergeant on the corner of Prudhoe Street, on the hour.'

Dad showed him to the door, and now Mrs Vicar was on her feet too. And Mrs Vicar's face was pale, and her lips trembled as she said, 'I shall have to tell my husband . . . I don't see how Miss Crimond can go on holding her secretaryship of the Board of Moral Responsibility after this . . . oh, I do so *hate* trouble and voices raised . . .'

And for the first time since his whole plan had worked so well, Billy felt sorry and guilty. Mrs Vicar was such a love, and she was so upset and trembling. His gang would just laugh, and not care about Mrs Vicar at all. But God would be watching . . . God saw everything. God would want an explanation . . .

But Dad, after Mrs Vicar had gone, waltzed around the room like a two-year-old, flicking the gold sovereign up in the air and catching it, and yelling, 'Three weeks' rent, three weeks' rent . . . I'll just nip down to the shop for an ounce of baccy, and some sweets and mebbe . . .'

'Baccy and sweets will do, William,' said Mam, a sudden catch of severity and fear in her voice.

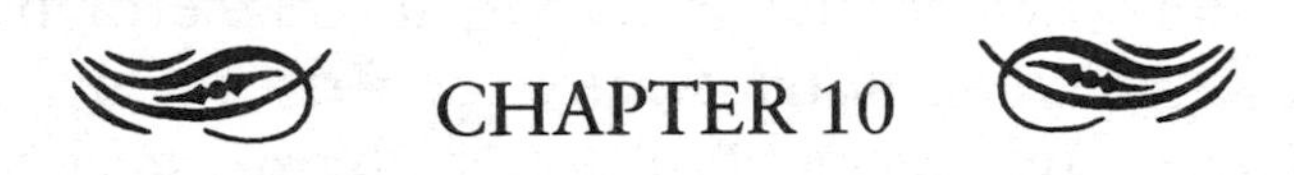

CHAPTER 10

The Night Mare

That night, Billy heard them. The Midnight Mechanics. Normally he never heard them, because he was a sound sleeper, and they never came till after midnight, when all decent folk were in bed.

But tonight the back of his head, with the bruise still as big as a hen's egg, kept throbbing painfully, in spite of the butter and witch-hazel Mam had put on it. It hurt every time he turned over, and that kept waking him up. He had eaten too many jelly babies, and sucked too much sherbet, because Dad had been generous with his new-found riches; and he felt a bit sick. Not sick enough to go down to the kitchen and *be* sick into the sink, but sick enough to lie and toss.

Still, he kept thinking of Miss Crimond's great defeat and giggling to himself, so it was quite cheerful.

Until he heard the sound of the Midnight Mechanics. The hatches in the back lanes slamming, boom, boom, boom, louder and louder, nearer and nearer. The dreadful clang of the buckets. And then the light of their lanterns coming through the curtains onto the whitewashed ceiling, and the strange gutteral inhuman calls they made to each other.

At this point, any child awake hid quickly under the bedclothes. Because they were part of what all children knew, like Santa Claus and Guy Fawkes. Every child knew that, dealing in unmentionable filth, They were destroyed by their dreadful work. They got unmentionable diseases. Their faces were eaten away by disease, so that their skulls showed through. Their eyes dropped out, one after another. Their fingers dropped off and then their hands and then their whole arms. But still they had to go on, one-armed, with their dreadful work, because it was the only trade they ever knew. By daylight, they crept back to their lairs and hid from the blessed light of day. They were misshapen; their wives, from contact with them, were as bad, and even their children were born misshapen, condemned never to go to school, but follow the same dreadful trade.

Billy was no braver than all the rest. But he was just putting his head under the bedclothes, when he heard the gentle whinny of a horse, and the soft slow clop of hooves, and rumble of wheels.

They had a horse with them. Of course, a horse to pull the Dreadful Cart. A poor horse who didn't deserve such a fate. Perhaps the poor horses got the diseases too? Billy could have wept, because he loved horses beyond all things, even beyond cricket. Never a horse came into Back Tennyson Street but Billy was out to it, with a lump of sugar or a wrinkled carrot nicked from Mam's larder. The dairyman's horse, the greengrocer's horse, even the rag-and-bone man's horse were personal friends. Billy would stroke their soft noses, and feel their warm grassy breath on his hand, and smell the strong smell of them, and peer inside their old leather blinkers at the great shining eyes, like dark limpid jewels.

Horses were magic and memory. When Grandpa had been rich, he had had two fine matched black horses, Jet and Satan, to pull his carriage. Dad, in the days of his glory, had ridden to hounds many times. Horses were wealth, freedom, the open fields with the drab pavements of Back Tennyson Street left far behind. In Mam's secret Japanese box there was a tiny photograph of her, in the secret compartment, wearing a black riding habit and bowler hat. Riding side-saddle . . .

Billy hovered, between fear and desire. If he got out of bed onto the freezing lino, and parted the old velvet curtains, he would see scenes of unmentionable horror. But he would also see a new horse. And even if he saw scenes of horror, he would be the first boy who had ever looked upon them in living memory. He could just see his gang's faces tomorrow, when he said the words, 'I've *seen* the *Midnight Mechanics*!'

And then he could wring their withers with gory descriptions, and make the Mechanics out to be even worse than they really were, because nobody else would have seen them, nobody would dare contradict.

And nobody would ever dare challenge his leadership again. He would be a *hero*!

So he slipped out of bed, and put on his faded dressing gown, that had once been red and came down to his feet, and was now pale pink and above his knees. Shivering with cold and excitement, he crept to the window.

Mid-November had put pretty frost-flowers all over it. Cursing, he breathed and breathed, scrubbed and scrubbed with the cuff of his dressing-gown. Again and again, the ice froze. In the end, he gave up. But he could see through the glass blearily now. There was the Dread Cart, with its high spoked wheels, and, for some reason, a tall post at every corner. From each post, even on this freezing night, topcoats hung. They must find it hot work, emptying those buckets, running to and fro, and never daring to spill a drop.

And there was the horse, right opposite to him, a ghostly grey in the light of the solitary lantern. And he immediately fell into love and sorrow, because in spite of its degradation, it was a beautiful horse, dappled and slender. What his father would have called a 'lady's hack', for he could see it was a mare. It almost had the slender lines of a racehorse, quite unlike the shaggy brown barrel-bodied beasts that usually pulled carts. Even a touch of Arab . . . well, no, he didn't know what an Arab looked like, but it was a phrase of praise his father sometimes used. But . . . a lady in distress, a lady who had seen better days. Like himself, like his own family. His heart went out to her; she looked half-starved, weary, pulling that awful thing, among these dreadful creatures.

But where *were* the dreadful creatures? He looked up the street both ways. There they were, sitting on a garden wall, under a still-lit lamppost. One of them was even smoking a pipe, and two had lit up cigarettes. Just like ordinary people. One seemed to be drinking from the lid of a tea-can . . . he could see no sign of dread disease . . . .

Avid for horror, he breathed and rubbed the window more frantically. But now he could see them clearer, he could see they still had all their arms and legs. None of their noses were eaten away; they still had lips to draw on fags or sip tea. In fact, apart from being brawny, they seemed in all matters to be perfectly ordinary men in caps, with their sleeves rolled up. In fact, he was almost certain he had seen one of them before, shopping round the town with his wife. He only lived a couple of streets away.

That was it! That was why nobody ever saw them in daylight. In daylight, they dressed up as ordinary people. But they must never tell anyone what their job was. They would just say they were on the night shift somewhere.

It is a sad fact that when some horror drains away, the world seems very grey and empty and flat. The Midnight Mechanics were no more real than Jack Frost or Santa. *Not* as real as Count Dracula. Billy had sudden doubts about Count Dracula too. But the thought was unbearable, and he thrust it away.

But now the monsters had turned into mere men, all his thoughts were for the horse. He noticed how her ribs showed through her thin hide, in the light of the lantern. How she nervously changed back feet every minute or so, standing on first one, then the other. She must be underfed, mistreated . . . He had a sudden urge to run downstairs to comfort her, to give her something to eat . . . But even as he thought this, the men further up the road dimped their fag-ends and began walking back to work.

He watched while they rumbled off round the corner, past the Misses Crimond's house. The Misses Crimond had the end of the terrace, which was always the poshest house, most sought-after, and costing an extra sixpence a week rent if you got one, because it was a little bigger, and had a front garden on two sides. But the Misses Crimond's father had built their house bigger still, with three bedrooms instead of two . . . a real little palace, the women said.

He got back into bed, shivering. And then decided.

Next week he would be ready for them. Fully dressed under his pyjamas. With a brown-paper carrier-bag full of old apple cores, wizened carrots, and even some grass he'd go down to the football field to pick.

CHAPTER 11

Making a Splash

'Nobody's talking to them any more,' said Sam Spode. 'People are crossing the street to stay out of their way.'

'And they weren't in church on Sunday,' said Nat, who was a choir boy and looked misleadingly angelic in his surplice and cassock. Like Satan before his great fall, Billy thought.

'Not on Sunday morning, nor Sunday afternoon, nor Sunday evening,' Nat added. He was proud of going three times a day though he said he hadn't believed in God since he was seven.

'Everyone's sent them to Coventry,' said Henry.

'That's a lie for a start,' said Albert, trying to get his two-penn'orth in. 'I saw them going shopping just this morning.'

Nobody tried to explain to Albert what 'sending to Coventry' really meant. Life was too short.

'It was a good plan that of yours, Billy,' said Nat. 'But it hasn't worked. I don't think anything will shift them. They'll never move down Tynemouth with the nobs.'

'But if they're going to Coventry,' said Albert, 'us *will* be shot of 'em.'

'Give 'im a kick, somebody,' said Billy. 'I can't be bothered. In the gob, for preference. Shut him up.'

'Let's go an' play football in Northumberland Park,' said Sam. Northumberland Park was a hopeless place to play football, being a narrow steep valley entirely covered in trees, flower-beds, rockeries and bowling-greens for old gaffers. The only point of playing football on its narrow tarmacked paths was that it was forbidden.

'Gerroff,' said Henry. 'That ain't no fun any more. They've given old Porkie the keeper the sack, 'cos he couldn't run fast enough to catch us. The new feller can run like hell. He can't half clout you an' all.' He nursed his ear, lost in unpleasant memory.

'Haven't you got *any* ideas, Billy?' asked Nat. 'You're just sitting there dreaming, you dozy sod. What's the matter with you?'

Billy smiled, a secret smile.

'I had a night mare,' he said, almost to himself.

'What?' asked Henry, who was a thoughtful child. 'You mean like Dracula sucking blood out of your neck and the Wolf Man chewing off your leg and Frankenstein's monster coming to pull you in bits? I dream that every night . . .' Henry was privileged because his grandpa worked the projector at the town's only cinema, and some thought he saw too many silent horror films.

'No,' said Billy dreamily, 'a different sort of nightmare.'

'Tell us about it!'

'Later,' said Billy, 'later.' Leadership had its privileges.

* * *

Billy heard the distant chimes of the parish church clock striking midnight. It jolted him out of the start of a dream about Jack the Ripper. It wasn't a frightening dream, because he knew the Ripper didn't rip boys. What was more, Billy, and Billy alone in the world, knew who the Ripper was: the Mayor of Tynemouth, and Billy was busy tracking him to his lair in the council chamber, with six stout policemen at his back. World fame at last!

But this was no night for dreaming. This was the night for the Midnight Mechanics, the night the night mare came. Billy bit his own wrist hard, to avoid drifting back to sleep. Would they *never* come? He felt hot, sweaty and uncomfortable, in his day clothes under his pyjamas. Like a mummy in its tomb, in the blackness of the bedroom. He reached under the bed, to make sure his bag of goodies for the horse hadn't moved, and felt the cold comforting rim of the chamber-pot instead.

Then he heard the first distant boom-boom of hatches.

He leapt out of bed so quick he felt sick. Then tiptoed onto the landing, listening for the soothing sound of parental snores. His mother snored softly, very like herself. His father's snores rose and fell dramatically, like the voice of a villain in a melodrama at the old Theatre Royal; still full of quarrels with the world. In their sleep, they sounded like they were still talking to each other, like in the daytime.

He tiptoed downstairs, straddle-legged, feet on the ends of every stair, so they wouldn't creak; his shoes in one hand, the bag of goodies in the other.

Only when he was putting his shoes on, crouching on the doormat, did he realise he was still wearing his pyjamas like an idiot. It took ages to wrestle out of them, and the booms and bangs getting nearer all the time.

The big key turned easily in the front-door lock. He'd oiled it three times the previous week; so much that Mam in her weekly cleaning had found trails of oil running down the inside of the front door, which had nearly given away the whole scheme, and taken all Billy's acting ability to explain away. He still didn't think Mam believed they had been doing lessons on oiling machinery in school; she said it was not the kind of thing schools taught, and damn right she was. But she'd supposed, with a deep sigh, that Billy was just trying to be helpful. Only, next time Billy felt helpful, would he give her plenty of warning?

Kicking his discarded pyjamas into the corner, he opened the front door on the cold of the night. The sound of rumbling wheels and clopping hooves was coming up their street now.

With trembling fingers, and dropping the bag twice, he transferred the key to the outside of the door and locked it. He didn't want any icy draughts creeping through Mam's open bedroom door; Mam could feel a draught in a heat-wave . . . Then he crouched under the shelter of the hedge, and listened to the cart draw up and stop. His nose would've told even a blind and deaf man that the Midnight Mechanics had arrived.

They were talking to each other, just like ordinary people.

'What's the matter, Ted?'

'Aah hung me coat on the cart, an' its dropped into the doin's.'

'Hard luck. But there's no point fishin' for it. It'll be no use to you now.'

'Aah knaa that. But it's got me sandwiches in the pocket . . .'

They drifted away up the street to eat their sandwiches and drink their tea, well clear of the awesome smell. Billy saw his chance, while their backs were turned. He'd have to be quick. Once they sat down on their favourite wall, they might turn their heads and see him any time. He didn't bother to open the gate, because it always gave a loud creak. He vaulted the low hedge, caught his toe in a stray sprig of privet, almost fell, and wildly flailing his arms, crashed across the street within inches of the night mare's nose.

Now she had already been aware of his lurking presence, though the men had not. It made her nervous. She was not like the horses of the day, the milkman's horse or the greengrocer's horse, used to being fed titbits and mucked about by hordes of kids. She was a creature of the empty silent night, used only to her handlers, and otherwise left in peace. So the arrival of this flailing monster, appearing suddenly round the rim of her blinkers . . .

She thought her last moment had come. She went from a standstill to a full gallop in five yards, her iron-shod hooves striking fearsome sparks from the road. The cart was no burden to her; the night was yet young. It was not a quarter full. She fled for the safety of her humans. Who let themselves fall backwards over the garden wall and so avoided utter annihilation. The street corner neared, and even in her panic, she knew the road to home and safety. A sharp right turn outside the Misses Crimond's house. The cart's iron-shod wheels screeched a firework display out of the kerbstones as it mounted the pavement. It nearly tipped over on its side then, but slowly righted itself as the corner approached. And then, as she swung hard right to take the corner, the front nearside wheel caught on the low wall of the Misses Crimond's house.

It seemed to Billy, staring aghast from down the street, that it was not so much a collision as an explosion. Under the dim distant rays of the street-lamp, the wooden planks of the cart flew everywhere, weakened and rotted by the corroding loads of years. But it was the tidal wave of contents that leapt the Misses Crimond's low hedge, enveloped the shining windows in the blinking of an eye; some lighter particles even seemed to hover over the chimney pots, against the dark night sky . . .

Billy did not wait to see more. Even before the noise of the crash had finished echoing up and down Back Tennyson Street, he slipped through the front door and locked it, and fled up the stairs in a muddle of bag, shoes and crumpled pyjamas.

'What's that, hinny?' The sound of Mam's sleepy voice came faintly to him as he tucked the tell-tale bag into bed, threw his clothes onto his chair in no worse a disarray than usual, and pulled the covers up to his chin, trembling with cold and terror.

'Drunks again,' said Dad, and rolled over, making

the bedsprings creak like a ship in a storm.

Billy lay shivering, not wanting to face the morrow.

'By heck,' said Nat, lost in wonder, 'there's even blobs of it up on the gable end. And on that little spike-thing on top.'

A large and admiring crowd stood in a semicircle, warily upwind, blocking the whole street.

'Look,' said Henry. 'You can see the marks where the cart mounted the pavement. Something must have scared the horse out of its wits.'

'And if the horse was *used* to seeing the Midnight Mechanics, it must have been something *terrible* to have scared it like that.'

'You mean, like Dracula?' said Sam Spode hopefully. 'What do you think, Billy?'

Billy said nothing. Just watched the big fat police sergeant making notes in his little book, while a bloke with spectacles, who was said to be from the council, went on and on. Billy's only thought was how soon would they come to arrest him? And where would he be sent away to as a punishment? And would Mam be allowed to come and see him and bring him a cake with a file hidden inside, so he could escape and run away to sea?

But he stood there with the others for ages, and nobody as much as looked at him. Everyone was too busy saying they'd heard the crash, but thought it was some accident down Smith's Dock. Like a ship falling over through carelessness . . .

'The first thing they knew at the stables,' said the man from the council, 'was the horse appearing with just the harness dangling. Damn near knocked the stable gates down. It's not injured. Just worn out. It's normally such a placid horse . . . a bit past its work, even. Weary and slow.'

'It passed my constable in Prudhoe Street like a bleeding rocket. Said it would have won the Derby. Point is, what scared it?'

'My blokes haven't a clue. Too busy saving their own skins.'

The man's words were like manna in the wilderness. For the first time since he'd got up that morning, Billy began to breathe from the bottom of his lungs. Even, amidst the stench that arose from the Misses Crimond's garden, he began to feel hungry again after having left his breakfast entirely untouched, which Mam blamed on the smell that was leaking through every crack in the doors and windows, far worse than the guano-works down by the river.

'Horses is queer cattle,' said the sergeant. 'I don't suppose we'll ever find out.'

Oh, thought Billy, life was so sweet!

But life was about to get even sweeter. A huge pantechnicon, pulled by two huge dray-horses, and hugely marked on the side: CARTER PATTERSON hove into view at the end of the street. It pulled up outside the Misses Crimond's. Then the man beside the driver said, awed, 'Lor lumme, we'll have to use the back door. I wouldn't use the front, not even for time and a half. You'd want danger money.'

The van backed cumbrously, went off round the corner, and the suddenly excited crowd followed.

And watched as the men carried out first aspidistras, then the little three-legged bamboo tables the aspidistras usually stood on. Then chairs, tables . . . then even a large, ancient and highly polished sideboard. Hope grew among the crowd, unbearably, and then, when they began to carry beds and wardrobes out from upstairs, a ragged cheer went up.

'They're going. They're *moving*. Permanent. Where you delivering to, mate?'

'Ten Grand Parade, Tynemouth,' said the man. 'If you haven't got any *objections*!'

'Objections?' Old Mrs Marday flung her arms around his neck and kissed him. 'Like a cup of tea, sonny?'

'Don't mind if I do,' said the man. 'Two sugars, and two for me mate as well.'

'You wouldn't rather have something stronger?' asked old Mr Faraday. 'A nice glass of Bass?'

'Or a whisky?' yelled somebody else.

'By God, Tom,' said the driver. 'Us is gettin' treated like royalty. When's Coronation Day, Missus?'

They hung around all day, the crowd, in the hopes of seeing the Misses Crimond. But of them there was no sign. Finally, when Billy had come back from school for his dinner, they saw the pantechnicon depart. Then the Misses Crimond's house was locked up by a large fat man, with a long grey raincoat and black bowler hat, and a wary but friendly expression.

Accosted by Mrs Marday, who had been to the forefront all morning, he said he didn't think the Misses Crimond were coming back ever.

'Who's going to collect the rents then?'

'I am,' said the man. 'I collect a lot of rents round

here, and I'm taking these on as well. And I like my money waiting ready, five o'clock Friday sharp. So I don't have to hang around. I've got too much to do. I come to the back door, so have it ready for me. Right?'

There was a huge cheer. No more poking and prying inside your houses. No more nosies with pursed lips. People embraced each other, like it was the end of the Great War, all over again.

'Well,' said the fat man, pleased at this unusual popularity. 'I've got another bit of good news for you an' all. The rents is coming down again.'

'*Coming down*?' Mrs Marday couldn't have been more incredulous if she'd been crowned Queen. 'I don't believe it. Why?'

''Cos the going rate for a house round here is five shillings a week, and no more. I told them ladies straight. Houses are coming vacant elsewhere, I said. One in Brannan Street, one in Mickleover Street. At five shillings a week. Why should folk stay here an' pay seven, I asked them? You'll soon have a street of empty houses, I said. What's the sense in that? What'll you live on then? They saw my point, I'm glad to say.'

If he hadn't been so fat, Billy thought the people would have carried him round shoulder-high, like the man who scored the winning goal.

It was a wonderful day. It was a wonderful night. Pocket-money restored. There would be roasts for Sunday lunch and cake for Sunday tea. And on the Saturday morning . . . football in the street. People stood at their front gates, watching, laughing, cheering them on. Even when the ball flew into their front gardens, they happily threw it back. Mr Miller even produced a very old *proper* football, which he said he'd used when he played for Percy Main Reserves. And he dribbled up and down the pavement four times, beating all comers, till he tripped over the kerb and cracked his head, and was led away by his wife, bleeding slightly but still grinning.

Altogether, a miraculous weekend. Until, at Sunday teatime, just before they were willingly called in for tea, because there was cake, Nat said for the hundredth time, 'I wonder what scared that horse.'

Billy took a deep breath and said, 'I did.'

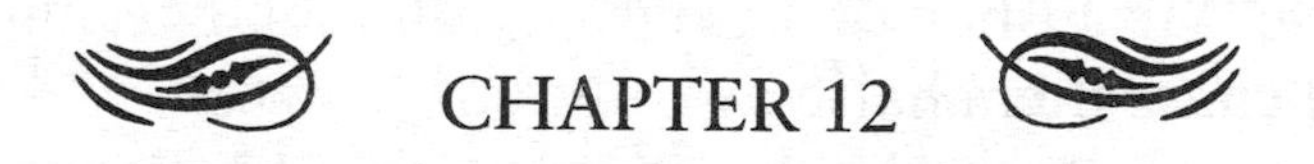

CHAPTER 12

The Midnight Mechanic

'Garn,' said Nat. 'Pull the other leg – it's got bells on it. You were nowhere near, that time o' night. Tucked up fast asleep in your little bed.'

And that was the verdict of them all. They all looked at Billy with sneering contemptuous faces.

It was not to be borne; to tell your deepest darkest most dangerous secret and not be believed. Billy was filled with rage. 'I was up an' dressed, waiting for them. I had a bag o' goodies for the horse. I saw them through the curtains, the week afore. The Midnight Mechanics.'

'So what do they look like then?' sneered Nat. 'No hair? Purple skin? A hole where their noses should be? This had better be good, you *liar*!'

'They were perfectly ordinary blokes. Look like everybody else. There's one of them lives two streets away – I think he's called Mr Fisher.'

'I know Mr Fisher,' said Henry thoughtfully. 'He does pong a bit funny. We went to his house carol singing last year, and when he came to the door, he ponged so funny we couldn't sing any more. But he gave us tuppence.'

'*Prove* it,' said Nat to Billy, a little doubt growing

in his voice.

So they marched to Mr Fisher's house there and then. In a body. Billy thinking very hard how he could put things. He knew it would be fatal to accuse Mr Fisher of being a Midnight Mechanic. He'd chase them halfway round the town . . .

But, halfway to Mr Fisher's house, a brilliant idea came to him. So he knocked on the door with a glimmer of hope.

Mr Fisher came to the door in a clean white shirt. It didn't have a collar attached, but the collar stud was brightly polished, and his braces were bright red with posh patterns on them, under his open waistcoat. His face was almost indecently clean and red, as if he'd been painfully scrubbing it. And his white hair was newly washed and fluffy, so it stood up like a cock's comb. But he still ponged funny, as Henry had said.

He surveyed the assembled expectant faces.

'Go on,' he said. 'Sing something then! "Hark the Herald" or summat. Though you're a bit early – the third of December. Still, I'm in a good mood.'

'No,' said Billy. 'We've come to thank the horse.'

'What horse? Haven't got no horse here.' Mr Fisher looked genuinely baffled, but still not at all cross.

'The horse that . . . did for . . . Miss Crimond.'

Mr Fisher laughed so heartily his eyes vanished inside rolls of skin. 'By God,' he choked at last. 'I never saw owt like it. Right to the top of the house. An' it's sent her packin' at last, I hear!'

'That's why we've come to thank the horse,' said Billy earnestly. 'We're all going to have a happy

Christmas, 'cos of that horse. We thought we'd bring it a few Christmas titbits – if we knew where it lived.'

He watched as the awful thought struck Mr Fisher. His face darkened ominously, with a mixture of fear and rage. Because his secret was out, staring everybody in the face. It was a situation that would have taxed the British Ambassador talking to Kaiser Bill, before the balloon went up, in the Great War.

'How should I know where that horse lives?' he shouted. 'Why should I know anything about that bloody horse? What you bin saying to people?'

'We only heard you were passing and saw the crash,' said Billy soothingly. 'And might have seen which way the horse galloped off afterwards. We're trying to track it down, see?'

'Who told you I saw the crash?'

Billy almost said, 'You did.' But that would not be helpful. 'Some old granny down our street,' he said vaguely.

'Old grannies – nosy old bitches. Ought to have more to do with their time than spy on people.'

'We're only trying to find the horse,' said Billy placatingly.

He looked at Mr Fisher, and Mr Fisher looked at him. The man knew his whole future hung in the balance. If his secret once got out . . . kids catcalling after him . . . he'd have to leave the district; he'd maybe have to leave town . . .

'Can you keep a secret?' he asked Billy.

Billy nodded vehemently. 'We all can.' All the rest nodded vehemently too.

'Well, I work on the night shift down on the Fish

Quay. I work all hours. So that's how I came to see the crash. And I often see the Midnight Mechanics goin' home in the dawn. So I know where that horse lives . . . you swear to keep it secret? Cross your heart and hope to die?'

They all solemnly crossed their hearts and hoped to die.

'They've got a stables and a little field on the road to Percy Main. A little place on the right where the houses stop. You know it?'

They all nodded, solemnly again, amazed at Billy's skill in lying.

'Mum's the word,' said Billy. 'Thank you very much.'

As Mr Fisher closed his front door, Billy had never seen such a look of worry on a grown-up's face.

'Cor,' said Nat. 'He *is* a Midnight Mechanic. We could'a *blackmailed* him. Sixpence a week for sure . . .'

'Blackmail,' said Billy piously, 'is a *crime*. You want to go to prison? Anyway, now he's a *mate* of ours, right? So keep your big trap shut, or I'll shut it for you.'

There was a murmur from the gang. That was enough to shut Nat's trap for ever.

They scurried towards home, eager for Sunday cake. Billy thought that without the Misses Crimond, and with the chance to see the night mare, it was going to be the best Christmas ever.

They went down to the stables straight after school on the Monday night. It was getting dark, but the stable door was open, and a lantern glowing inside. The four horses were champing on their hay, and it all looked a bit like the Christmas crib in church.

'What you lot want?' asked a suspicious grown-up voice behind them. A little old man was standing there, with very bandy legs inside a pair of horseman's leather leggings, and a short charred blackened pipe stuck in the corner of his mouth. They instantly thought him wonderful, because he had no teeth, and never took the pipe out of his mouth when he spoke, and they would have endless fun impersonating him afterwards.

Billy did his come-to-thank-the-horse routine again. And got the usual laugh at the expense of Miss Crimond. And then the same black look, as the man knew he'd given himself away.

But Gus, as he was called, had less to lose, less to worry about. He wasn't a Midnight Mechanic himself. Just an ostler who looked after the horses during the day. And he was old, and held his back frequently, and complained about his rheumatics; and was only too glad of the help they offered, to muck out and carry trusses of hay and bales of straw at weekends. They worked like slaves for two Saturdays, and didn't even think about asking for pay. There were so many wonders. There were mice who fled squeaking through the straw, and a hope of seeing rats, and Patch, Gus's old terrier, who had been a great ratter in her day, and still wasn't bad. And Gus told them how he'd once been a jockey, and come third in the Northumberland Plate, which everyone called the Pitman's Derby. And how he hadn't lost his teeth one by one, like any other old gaffer, but had had them all kicked out at once, by an angry horse.

The horses ponged a bit; but all horses pong a bit, and these were no worse than usual, only a bit different. There were four of them. The other three were stocky brown beasts, with barrel bellies, thick legs and shaggy fur, from being out in the open so much. One, called Trojan, was very bad-tempered, and famous for once biting the mudguard off a motor car, which cost the council a packet. Trojan was admired from a distance, because he had a lot of nasty tricks, like deliberately standing on your foot, or crushing you against the side of his stall with his big belly. But the other two, Neddy and Dobbin, were placid and friendly, and even let the lads sit on their backs while they grazed around the field. You couldn't call it riding exactly, because they did exactly what they wanted, whether there was anybody on their backs or not. But you could wear your six-gun and gunbelt, and your dad's old trilby hat, and pretend you were a cowboy.

But Billy cared nothing for Trojan, Neddy or Dobbin. Every spare moment he spent with his Night Mare, who was called, quite properly, Princess. She was nervous; she wouldn't let anybody ride her; but he just liked being with her, and imagining she was young again, and he was her jockey, and he was going to ride her in the Pitman's Derby. And win, of course.

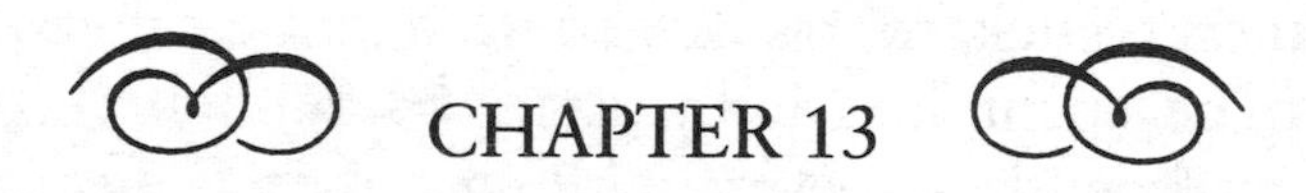

CHAPTER 13

Memories of Grandeur

'No little friends this afternoon?' asked Mrs Marjorie Mallory, opening the door to him and beaming at the lovely December sunset.

'I feel like a bit of peace and quiet,' said Billy. 'They're a bit of a handful . . . to keep under control.'

'Ah, Master William, you're just like your grandfather,' said Mrs Mallory fondly. 'A leader of men. He built his fortune up from nothing, you know.'

This news cheered Billy no end. He was getting a taste for the grand life: the long gravel drive, and marble statues in the garden, the smell of polish in the house, almost as strong as poison gas. Nice cakes for tea and . . . being polite and being treated like a gentleman. *Becoming* a gentleman. Though he supposed he had been *born* a gentleman. Mam had, locked away in her secret box, a silver spoon with his name on it, that she said was his christening spoon. He must have lived his first three years a gentleman. And then . . . disaster had struck.

'My father,' he said, 'was he a leader of men?'

Mrs Marjorie Mallory screwed her face up tight, as

if remembering gave her pain.

'Well,' she said at last, 'he had a lot of it. He got on well with everybody. He was very popular, like your grandpa. But . . . it was just that money wouldn't stick to his fingers. He no sooner had it than he spent it. Madly generous he was . . . with all his friends . . . even with any beggar he met in the street . . . no, it was the other two who could hang on to their money. Your Uncle Horace and your Uncle George. Very tight they were, always. In those days, your father used to give me a little Christmas present . . . something thoughtful, very thoughtful for a man. A set of lace-edged hankies, or a big bottle of scent from Paris. All I ever got off Horace or George was a half-crown in my hand, like I was the maid or something . . . if they thought on.' Her face darkened. 'It was as if your grandfather split in half in his sons. Horace and George got his gift of making money. Your dad got his gentlemanly ways. It's sad now, to see the way your dad's placed. But it would have been no good your grandfather leaving him money – even if he'd been left the lot, he'd have been as poor as a church mouse in a couple of years. Still, I'd have married *him*, if he'd asked me. I'd never have married Horace or George, not for all the tea in China. I could never stand a *mean* man.' Mrs Marjorie Mallory's face, just for a moment, dissolved into a sentimental look that wiped away all wrinkles and made her look almost young.

'But my grandpa . . .'

'He was like a prince – a king. He entertained the old king – Edward VII – to dinner once, you know.

As head of the Northumbria Lodge of the Freemasons, of which he was Grand Master. I'll bet those two had a lot to say to each other. They were so alike. I can imagine them sitting back smoking their cigars and drinking their port and laughing. It's a gift, being a good king. Half of it's *enjoying* being a king – our present one is such a solemn soul – he doesn't look like he enjoys being king very much. But the old king, and your grandpa, they could be pleasant with anybody, high or low. The common touch . . . yet nobody would dare to get over-familiar. Your grandpa had a *look* – it would silence Horace and George and your dad, even when they were quarrelling worst, even when they were grown men working in the business. A look from your grandpa – that was all it took. I'm glad I never saw that look. He was always very pleasant with me.'

She had not asked Billy in tonight. Instead, they were walking round the outside of the house, as if Mrs Marjorie Mallory wanted to enjoy the last of the sunlight. Or else to show him something. For they were going to a part of the grounds where he'd never been before. A high brick wall was blotting out the light coming through the bare sunset elms. A high brick wall with a round brick hole in it.

His heart leapt. The stables! The place where grandpa's matched pair of black horses, Jet and Satan, had lived. Where Dad and Mam must have mounted up, laughing, in their grand clothes, when the world was young . . .

Mrs Mallory pushed the great black gate open with difficulty. Billy had to help her.

'My present employers, the Jensons, care nothing for this. Mr Jenson has a motor car . . . a Daimler . . . great oily thing. Their chauffeur drove them down to Mentone in it . . . their boys are mad keen on motorbikes when they're not at school. We've not seen a horse since your grandpa died. But everything's still here. The tack room. Your grandpa's old carriage . . . wasn't worth selling, I suppose. There's even hay in the hayloft. They're narrow people, the Jensons, though nice enough. He's a big jeweller with shops in Newcastle and Sunderland, and even Edinburgh. He can afford to take the winter off, I can tell you. But there's not much life. They only keep six servants. Her maid and his man are away with them. In your grandpa's time the house was full of servants and three gardeners, too. Two full-time stable lads, for eight horses. All along here. See, their last nameboards are still up. Jet and Satan; Beauty, Salamander, White Blaze and Sapphire were hunters, and Dimble and Bumblebee were ladies' hacks.'

Billy could imagine the whole scene, the horses' heads curiously poking out of the half-open door, waiting for titbits; the stable lads busy grooming or shovelling manure in the old barrow that still stood bleaching in the sun, with a rusty shovel in it.

'I've seen your grandpa arm-wrestle with one of the stable lads,' said Mrs Mallory. 'Off with his jacket and waistcoat, and straight into it. Bet him a shilling he could beat him, he did. And lost. The lad was terrified, because your grandpa fell on his back in the horse muck at the end of it. But he got up laughing and just said to the lad: "Cheshire born,

Cheshire bred, strong in't arm, thick in't head" because the stable boy, Antrobus, was a Cheshire lad, see? Then he got both lads to dust him down, and gave him his shilling, and his mate sixpence for a drink, and walked off laughing. He was over sixty then, but those lads would'a *died* for him. They were heartbroken when he died instead. They both went back to Cheshire; couldn't stand it round here, after that.'

'Why would they have died for him, Mrs Mallory?'

'Because he understood them, understood what they needed, and gave it to them. Those uncles of yours, they may *look* like him, in their sour way, but all they care about is money. Nobody'd die for them; nobody likes them, not even their wives, they're afraid of life, and money's no cure for that. Whereas your grandpa always said "*carpe diem*". That's Latin for "Seize the day". He seized every day that came and enjoyed it, right to the end.'

Billy took a deep breath. 'If he understood what people needed . . . why didn't he understand about *us*?'

Mrs Mallory sighed. 'Maybe there was nothing he could do. Your mam was the one with sense there. But he couldn't leave things to her and not to your dad. Your dad would have died of shame, before the whole town. Maybe your grandpa was still trying to work that out, when he was taken from us. It was very sudden, of an Easter Monday. He just lay back in his chair after a grand day, lit up one of his cigars, sighed in contentment and had a heart attack. Within the day, he was dead. Just enough time to say his goodbyes.'

They had stopped walking, outside the open doors of the double coach house. On the right, there was just a nasty pool of oil, and tools, where the Daimler had stood. On the left, grey with dust and wisps of cobwebs, stood Grandpa's carriage, with its great wheels and big black oil lamps.

'I remember him sitting in that,' said Billy, suddenly. 'My mam held me up to him, and he gave me a kiss and sat me on his knee.'

'Powerful fond of you, he was, Master William. It's a pity he hadn't lived. You'd have had great talks, the pair of you. But each man has his time . . .'

'Eight years,' said Billy, bitterly. 'Eight years. That's all that was needed. Why did he only leave those bits of furniture: those chairs, the clock, that shovel?'

'He must have thought about it carefully,' said Mrs Mallory. 'They were his favourite things. His clock, his favourite chair, his dead wife's chair. He chose them carefully enough.'

'Had he any other sayings, apart from *carpe diem*?' asked Billy, still searching for something of value from the wreck.

'Aye,' said Mrs Mallory, her face convulsed with laughter. 'He always said, "The more you cry, the less you pee"'.

And laughing together enough to fall down, they went back to the house for a mug of cocoa and cakes.

Only Billy turned up at the stables on the Saturday before Christmas Eve, in the afternoon. The others had lost interest; there were relations to visit, and early mince-pies to consume, and presents in coloured paper, to be squeezed surreptitiously when no one was looking, to try to guess what was in them. But Billy had brought Christmas presents for Princess. Three real fresh carrots, not wizened ones, which Mam had given him specially. And even two old whole apples. Princess really enjoyed them.

'That's kind,' said old Gus, sitting watching Billy feed her. 'I'm glad she's getting a good send-off, for her last Christmas.'

'Last Christmas?' Billy whirled.

'Aye, poor old lass. She'd have gone already, if it hadn't been for Christmas . . .'

'Gone *where*?' There was something in Gus's voice that warned Billy that terrible news was coming.

'Oh, she's being sold,' said Gus. 'Just . . . sold.' Billy could tell he now wished he'd kept his mouth shut.

'Sold to who? Can I still go and see her, where she's going?'

'She's not going anywhere.' Gus was staring down at the straw.

Billy was frantic. Gus was just not making sense. He stood over Gus and shouted, 'Tell me, tell me!'

After a long time, Gus said wearily, 'She's going for horsemeat. To feed the pussy-cats. They're coming for her, day after Boxing Day. They'll get their last five quid of value out of her, trust them.'

'But . . . but . . . she's fit and well. Look at the way she enjoyed my carrots.' Billy heard his voice going up in a scream.

'She was never strong enough for hauling the

carts, really. It was never work she should've been put to. Them carts is terrible heavy, at the end of a shift. They've just knackered her.'

'But she's not old. Not that old. She could live for years.'

'Aye. If she had a kind owner, wi' money to burn, an' a little field to herself. Somebody who cared for her. But the bloody council doesn't care for nobody. Money's all they care about. They'd sell *me* for cat's meat, if they could.'

Billy just stood in agony.

'Go an' say goodbye to her then, lad! I know ye're fond of her.'

But Billy couldn't go near Princess now; he couldn't even look at her. All peaceful and trusting in her stable, and by the day after Boxing Day, she'd be bloody little pieces of meat on the cat's-meat man's barrow . . .

He turned and fled.

'Merry Christmas,' called Gus dolefully after him.

It was not to be borne. The innocent horse, the horse that had brought everyone a happy Christmas, his horse, his own personal night mare . . . he wandered in a daze. He had learned how the world wagged. He had finally learnt how it felt to be poor and powerless. He had learnt that he, and what he wanted, amounted to *nothing*. He even began to understand why Mam so often looked weary and beaten; why Dad drank and went crazy; or put his head in his hands and moaned.

He was nothing. At one point, he stopped still for

two whole minutes, in the middle of a street, so that passers-by and strangers stared at him. If he'd been a grown-up, people might have spoken to him, prodded him back to life, even fetched a policeman to see to him. But he was just a silly little kid, and nobody ever understood what silly little kids were up to . . .

But he was, deep within himself, making a vow. He would work and work at school; he would work and work in life, and one day he would be rich and famous. He didn't care at what. Just rich and famous. He would shout for people, and they would come running; he would pick up his telephone and ring the council, and ask them what the bloody hell they meant by it, and they would cower. He would be an alderman, a mayor. Like Uncle Horace and Uncle George.

Like Grandpa.

He started walking again. Because he knew where he was going now.

The Elms. Where the name Leggett still amounted to something. Mrs Marjorie Mallory would have money. She had to have money, to run the great house. At least five pounds. And there were empty stables behind The Elms. He'd seen them, he'd walked round them. And there was still hay in the lofts above the stables; plenty of hay. He would persuade Mrs Mallory . . . promise to work like a slave picking up leaves to pay for it all . . .

'I'm sorry, pet,' said Mrs Marjorie Mallory, for about the tenth time. 'There's nothing either you or I can do. That's life, Billy. Life is very hard. You'll learn that, as you get older.'

She had done her best. She had offered him ginger beer and fresh-baked mince-pies. She had cuddled him and let him cry.

But it was all useless. All he could see before his eyes was Princess, trusting, eating her carrots. And the smelly piles of meat he'd seen so often, unthinking, on the cat's-meat man's cart.

'You'd better go now, lovey,' said Mrs Mallory. 'It's starting to get dark. Your mam will be worryin'.'

'She'll be out shopping,' said Billy bitterly. 'Shopping and wishing everybody a Merry Christmas.'

But he got up to go. Else he would start crying again, and that wouldn't be fair on Mrs Mallory.

'Here,' she said, bustling round him, relieved to be free of the burden he'd become. 'Take these mince-pies for your mam. And . . .' she thought for a minute, and went into the posh drawing-room and felt inside an ornate box, 'here's a grand big cigar for your dad. Mr Jenson won't miss one – he smokes that many. And it'll remind your dad of the good old days . . .' On the front doorstep she gave him a last big hug and a smacking kiss. 'I wish I could wish you a Merry Christmas, pet. But I won't.'

He carried the mince-pies all the way home. He felt like throwing them in the gutter; just like Dad smashed plates one after the other, when he got really angry. But he didn't. They were Mam's mince-pies. Like the cigar rustling in his pocket in its big gold band was Dad's.

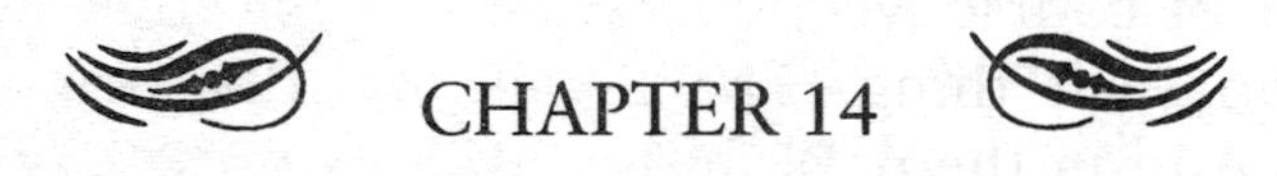

CHAPTER 14

The Chair

There was nobody in, when he got home. He had to pull up the front-door key through the letterbox on its string. Mam would be hours yet, and come back laden like a pack-horse. Dad much later, trying to be full of Christmas cheer on the tiny glass of sherry his boss would have given him, for working late without even getting paid for it . . .

The fire was low, nearly going out, but he made no attempt to mend it, or turn up the gas lamps over the mantelpiece. He just wanted to sit in the cold and dark and let misery sweep over him. He threw himself down in Grandpa's great chair, and as he did so, something rustled intriguingly in his inside pocket. He drew it out; Dad's Christmas cigar, in its cellophane wrapper. He played with the wrapper, his fingers quite pleased with the feel of it. Somehow it soothed his misery. And then it gave a kind of popping noise, and one end of the wrapping opened, and the smell of tobacco was overpowering and rich. A slight faint memory came to him, from earliest childhood. Of Grandpa, Magic Grandpa, leaning back in his great chair after dinner, unwrapping a cigar, and cutting off one end of it, and piercing the other, then lighting up and leaning back, his eyes shut, and face wreathed in contented smiles and smoke. Oh, Magic Grandpa, save us now! Me and my horse!

But of course Magic Grandpa, being long dead, did no such thing. There was just darkness and cold. And in the dark and cold, Billy grew envious of Grandpa, even *angry* with his silence.

Why should *you* have it all, and *us* have nothing?

It was then that the cigar tempted him, as strongly as one of Mam's infrequent boxes of Christmas chocolates, left lying open on the couch, unattended. Billy had a vision of himself lying back in Grandpa's chair, smoking that big cigar. Knowing, for a few moments, how it felt to be rich and powerful.

I mean, Dad didn't even *know* he had a big cigar for Christmas. He would never *need* to know . . . . In a second, Billy went from total despair to a sort of wild excitement. Nothing mattered but the big cigar now (though he had never as much as puffed a cigarette with Nat, who nicked the occasional one from his dad's packet of twenty when it was pretty full).

Of course, it wasn't the same as Grandpa. Grandpa had had a silver tool that he took from his pocket, to cut off one end of the cigar, and pierce the other. Billy had to cut and pierce with Mam's long thin dressmaking scissors. But he managed it OK. Then Mam's matches from the kitchen stove. With the third match, and much sucking, the end of the cigar finally glowed like a little red fire in the dusk of the room. He lolled back. So this was how it felt to be rich . . . ?

Actually, it began to feel not very nice. It began to feel a bit dizzy. The room began to whirl around a bit, round Billy's head. Sudden warm worms crawled in Billy's stomach. But with the vision of Grandpa's beatific smile before him, Billy persisted. It must only be a matter of *practice* . . .

The next second, he was running wildly for the kitchen sink, all thoughts of cigars fled from his mind.

He was very very sick. It just kept surging through him like tidal waves in the South Pacific. For a long time he just hung on, panting, to the edge of the sink. With streams of sweat running down the back of his neck and behind his knees. And his only thought was amazement, that his belly should hold so much.

It was only when it was all over, when he was clinging to the sink, vaguely glad to have survived, like a shipwrecked sailor on a raft, that he smelt the smell of . . .

Burning. Smoke. Smoke that came drifting into the kitchen and hung up by the ceiling like a dim grey blanket. It must be the chimney smoking . . . the wind must be in the wrong quarter tonight, as Mam sometimes said. But surely never as bad as this? He looked through the door of the living room, and it seemed to him the smoke was coming from Grandpa's chair . . .

He was there in one terrified bound. The cigar, that horrible cigar, lay still on the seat of Grandpa's chair, where he must have dropped it. Only a worm of fat white ash now, and around it, the old red velvet was well alight, a glowing edge that crept outward round a black crater in the seat of the chair, like an invading army.

He grabbed his cap and beat at it frantically. Glowing worms flew into the air in all directions. Yet still other glowing worms crept out across the velvet; there was no stopping them. With a howl he fled back to the kitchen for a jug of water.

That did it. The glowing worms went out, leaving a dreadful grey-black sodden mess. Billy stood with the empty jug in his hand, wishing, just wishing, the world would end. While from the end of the street, the faint sweet voices of the Salvation Army carol singers carolled:

'Glad tidings of great joy we bring
To you and all mankind.'

If Billy had had a gun, a real gun, he would have walked up to the end of the street and shot them.

But fortunately for all, he had no gun. And so he saved all his rage for a solitary wisp of smoke that still, after all that water, coiled up from the blackened seat of the chair. He snatched at it, with his bare fingers, to *pinch* it out, he was that *angry*.

It seemed to be coming from something white in the stuffing of the chair. White? Chair stuffing, as he well knew from many a Guy Fawkes' bonfire, was a miserable dreary browny-grey. He snatched at the tuft of white. It was stiff . . . like paper. White paper with a charred and still smoking edge.

He tugged at it viciously, and it began to draw out of the chair's depths. White paper with curling black lines on it. Writing.

A secret message from Grandpa? After all these

years? He scanned the curling black letters.

I promise to pay the bearer . . .

He knew what it was, because he'd seen one before. Once. Silly little Miss Watts, his teacher in the first year, had been sent one for her twenty-first birthday, and shown off by waving it in front of every class she could lay her hands on. Part of their education, she had said. Fat lot of chance any of them had of ever seeing another . . .

A five-pound note. Two and a half weeks' wages for Dad.

The price of Princess! He had wild thoughts of dashing back to the stables and buying her off Gus there and then. Mrs Marjorie Mallory would *have* to take her in. There was plenty of hay for her, in the stables at The Elms.

Only another lurking wisp of smoke saved him from madness. He plunged his hand down the charred hole after it. And found something else that crackled. Another note. No, one, two, three, four, five, six, seven, eight, nine, ten . . . with an elastic band holding them together. Fifty pounds, six months' wages . . . oh, glory. And still the wisp of smoke persisted, leading him on like the pillar of smoke led Moses by day. And his digging hand entered a stratum of pure bundles of paper . . .

'Billy, whatever are you up to?' Mam, standing in the doorway with two huge shopping bags in each hand, and a look of pure horror on her face.

He ran to her, shrieking words he couldn't get out properly, and waving a white bundle of paper in her face.

'Billy!' she shrieked back. 'What've you done – robbed a bank?'

They sat limp, exhausted, each side of the table, with the note-strewn velvet tablecloth between them. Billy did a last sum, on the edge of last Sunday's *News of the World* which Dad bought in spite of Mam's disapproval.

'Seven thousand, eight hundred and twenty-five pounds, Mam! We're *rich.*' Billy threw a handful of notes into the air, then quickly caught them again as they fluttered down. His mind, similarly, tried to wrap itself around what 'rich' meant. He tried turning it into sweets, then rent, then suits at the Fifty-Shilling Tailor's for Dad. But none of it would work. All he could think of that meant anything was that if Dad worked for seventy-eight more years, he wouldn't earn this much money.

He looked at his mother. But she was looking at the poor, burnt, soaking, gutted armchair. All its glory was gone; it looked like something dead, something murdered.

'Poor old thing,' said Mam. Then she said, 'It must have been his secret hoard. Uncle Horace and Uncle George always reckoned he had a secret hoard. They searched everywhere, but they never found it.'

Then she said to herself, 'He knew what he was doing. If your dad had got this when he died, he'd have blued the lot in a twelve month. Drink, horses, his awful cadging friends . . . He had to learn the value of money, like your grandpa said. By hardship . . .'

Mam's face grew even sadder. She shook her head in grief.

'But he's not learnt, Billy. Your dad's not learnt. Money still runs through his fingers like water. Dear God, this will send him totally off the rails.' She jumped to her feet, wringing her hands. 'We must hide it again, Billy. Where he'll *never* find it . . .' Billy had never seen her so frantic. 'Come on, help me, Billy. Go and fetch that sack from the wash-house. We can hide it in that. He never goes in there. But we'll know it's there. For a rainy day. It will be a blessing, Billy. I'll never have to lie awake and worry about money again . . .'

'But, Mam . . . the horse . . .'

'What horse?'

He burst into tears. And then, while she cuddled him, he told her all about Princess.

When he had finished, she started to her feet wildly. She had always loved horses, just like he had. But he could see she was caught between the devil and the deep blue sea. She wrung her hands; she paced up and down. He had never seen anyone in such agony, and he remembered his grandpa saying, 'Money can't buy happiness.'

And then it was too late. For Dad's footsteps, with that loose clinking boot heelplate, were coming up the back yard.

'By God,' said Dad at last, running his hands through the notes on the table again. 'The old devil! So that's what he meant!' He took another swig from the glass by his hand. It was brandy, which Mam kept for remedial purposes, like people fainting. But it had gone tonight. Though it was only a small bottle . . . Dad was only a bit tight, but then the pubs weren't open yet. 'We shall live like *Kings*, young Billy-me-lad.' He reached over and slapped Billy on the back painfully. 'We'll *show* the bastards how Leggetts ought to live! Like gentlemen! Not like our money-grubbing Horace and our tight-fisted George. When my old mates hear about this, that'll pin their lugholes back. Oh, we'll be the talk of the town! Just you wait and see!' He took another swig. 'An' wait till Monday morning. I'll go right into the dock manager's office an' tell him he can stuff his rotten little pay-clerk's job where it'll hurt most! Eight years of swallowing insults from that bounder . . .'

The silence from the other side of the table, Mam's side, was like the silence of the tomb.

'What's up wi' ye, Maggie? Cat got your tongue?'

Mam looked so pale, Billy thought she was going to faint. But finally, she took a deep breath and said, 'It's not *your* money!'

'Course it's my bloody money. My father left me the chair.'

'And what about the two thousand my father settled on *me*, when we married? My money, that you boozed and gambled away, after your father died?'

A shifty look came into Dad's eyes. You could tell he felt bad about that. Suddenly he grabbed up handfuls of notes and threw then at Mam. 'Tek your bloody father's money. I hope it chokes you.'

'And what about *him*?' said Mam, pointing at Billy. 'Doesn't he get any? For his education? For a good school, like you went to?'

Again, Dad looked shifty. He said loudly, 'No son of mine goes wi'out good schooling.'

'Right,' said Mam, gathering up money. 'Two thousand for me, and three thousand for him. Right?'

'You'd bleed a man dry,' said Dad. 'You wouldn't even let a man have enough left to have a drink with his friends.'

'And I will tell you now, I'm leaving you, William. I'm not going to sit around here and watch you drink yourself nigh to death in idleness. I went through that once before, and I'll not go through it again.'

Billy stared aghast. Not only were his parents going to part, his universe explode, but before his very eyes, the embattled figure of his mother grew taller, and his great big father grew smaller.

'Tek it all, blast you,' screamed his father, throwing bundles of notes at his mother with real hate.

'Thank you' said Mam, tight-lipped. 'I will.' And she began stuffing it all into a leather shopping bag.

'I'm going out to get drunk,' said Dad. He scooped up a couple of notes that were still blowing about, and slammed out of the house.

Mam collapsed into her chair and burst into tears.

'Mam,' said Billy, full of horror at all the wreckage he'd caused. 'We're not going to leave him, are we? Not at *Christmas*?'

Mam took his hand gently. 'It's all right, Billy. I wasn't crying because I'm going to leave him. I'm crying wi' the strain of standing up to him. For the first time ever, I stood up to him. After all these years. An' he collapses like a paper bag. It'll be all right now, Billy. Oh, he'll come back roaring like a wild beast. But we shan't be here. We are going to stay in an *hotel*. And have a grand Christmas dinner. In fact, I think we'll stay at the Grand at Tynemouth. And the money can go in the manager's safe. And after Christmas, we go to the bank.'

'But me Dad . . .'

'By Boxing Day, he'll be as gentle as a lamb. Making all sorts of promises. Which I shall *hold* him to. I am going to be a lady again, Billy, and you are going to be a gentleman.'

Billy thought he quite liked the idea of being a gentleman. But before that . . .

'The horse, Mam. The horse. *Princess*!'

'Oh,' said his mother. 'We must look after Princess. I owe a lot to Princess. Without you and her, I would never have had the courage to stand up to your dad. I shall go and see your Gus tomorrow. It's going to be quite a Christmas Eve.'

'But me Dad?'

She smiled, seraphically. 'There'll be other Christmas Eves, Billy. But there'll be no stopping him this one.

'Now go and change into your Sunday suit. You're going to take a lady out to dinner. You must look your *best*.'

And something new in the way she held her head told him it was all going to come true.

Carpe diem: Mam had seized the day.

They walked, with their bags, the short walk to

the station. There, they got an old black taxi, that smelled overpoweringly of leather. All the way to Tynemouth, Billy thought about Magic Grandpa. Who had come to the rescue after all. It was almost as if Magic Grandpa had foreseen what was going to happen. With Mam, with Dad . . .

With himself. As if, understanding their true natures . . . Dad's fecklessness, yearning to be loved, Mam's standards . . . his own nosiness . . . as if knowing all, Magic Grandpa had planted that money like a bomb, waiting to go off and change their world. Perhaps he had done it with faith, perhaps only with a wild gambler's hope. Mrs Mallory had told him Grandpa liked an occasional flutter at twenty-to-one.

Well, the flutter had paid off.

And he himself was resolved to seize the day. He had begun seizing it quite a bit recently. And he meant to go on.

Mind made up, Billy prepared himself, for his first dinner as a gentleman.